The Usborne Book of
Christmas Stories

First published in 2004 by Usborne Publishing Ltd., Usborne House, 83-85 Saffron Hill, London EC1N 8RT, England. www.usborne.com

Collection edited by Anne Finnis.
This selection and arrangement copyright © Usborne Publishing, 2004.

Cover illustration by Alan Marks.
Cover design by Russell Punter.
Inside illustrations copyright © Ian P. Benfold Haywood.
Designed by Hannah Ahmed.

A CIP catalogue record for this book is available from the British Library.

ISBN 0 7460 5845 4

Printed in Great Britain.

Contents

Stephen's Feast

Jean Richardson

Stephen could hear impatient voices calling his name as he crouched in his hiding place. The others would never find him here, he thought proudly.

He would show them he was just as clever as they were – as the youngest and smallest page in the palace, he was always being teased.

"Where has the boy got to?" That was a voice Stephen feared. "Trust him to vanish just when he's needed. What am I to tell the king? We can't find his page because he's playing hide-and-seek?"

The KING! Stephen's heart thudded at the news that the king wanted him. So far, Stephen had seen the king only from a distance.

Why should he want him now? And today of all days, when it was Stephen's birthday and the Feast of the saint after whom he was named. Having a birthday so close to Christmas meant only one set of presents, but this year Stephen didn't mind. The feasting and celebrating that went on in the palace were far grander than any birthday party could ever be.

Anxiously Stephen slipped out of his hiding place and presented himself to the angry chamberlain.

"About time! Don't you know you must never keep the king waiting? Hair like a haystack, filthy as a cellar rat! Clean yourself up, boy."

King Wenceslas was sitting by the window, looking out across the square.

"Come over here, boy," he called, "and tell me what you see."

Stephen obeyed him, wondering what he was supposed to say. Surely the king knew only too well what lay outside his own palace.

It was getting dark, and at first all Stephen could see was a blanket of snow, deep and crisp and even because no one had ventured out.

"That's a man, isn't it?" the king said, pointing to a dark shape in the snow. "Do you know who it is?"

Stephen was too far away to see the man's face, but he knew who it was. The man was often in the square, and Stephen and the other boys used to make fun of him. Only last week Stephen had thrown a snowball at him.

"I think –" he hesitated. "They say he's a poor man who lives on the other side of the forest, near St. Agnes' fountain. He comes looking for things...firewood...and scraps from the kitchen."

The king looked thoughtful. "Does he indeed. Well,

today I'm going to give him a surprise. And you're going to help me."

"Why me?" Stephen thought crossly as he got ready. "What a stupid idea – even if it was the king's – to take food and drink and logs to some miserable peasant who lived far away."

He pulled on his new fur boots – a present from his mother – and thought longingly of the games he would be missing, of the great fire of logs hissing in the servants' hall, of the spit on which a whole ox was roasting.

As he wrapped his cloak around him, the very thought of the snow making him shiver, he wondered whether he should take his new hunting knife. It was his proudest possession. With it in his belt he felt like a man. And who knew what dangerous animals might lurk in the forest?

The cook had loaded a small sledge with food and drink, and Stephen pulled it behind him. He could still smell the wonderful aroma of the roast meat. The cook had promised to save him some, but Stephen longed to stay in the Great Hall with its warmth and music and laughter.

The king led the way, carrying a sack of logs on his shoulder. The snow came up to Stephen's knees in places and the icy wind brought tears to his eyes. It raised clouds of loose snow, so that Stephen couldn't see where he was going. Suddenly he stumbled and fell. He called out in frozen fear when he realized the snow threatened to bury him.

"I want to go back," he sobbed. "I'm frightened. I can't go on any more."

The king lifted him up, dusted off the snow, and rescued the sledge. The frosted fur of his hat and beard glittered in the moonlight. He might have been a great bear.

"Courage, my little page," he said, and his voice was gentle. "You'll find it easier if you follow in my footsteps. The wind's cold enough to freeze your blood, but you'll soon thaw out when we get there."

They set off again, and this time Stephen was careful to tread in the king's footprints. He was right, it was easier to walk on the trodden snow.

He would have liked to ask the king why he cared about the peasant, but he hadn't enough breath to shout above the winter's rage. It occurred to him that the peasant must have wanted food and firewood very badly to venture out on such a bitter night. At the thought of how surprised and pleased the man would be, Stephen began to feel warmer.

Suddenly something gleamed ahead of them, and as they drew nearer, they saw an extraordinary sight. St. Agnes' fountain had been transformed into a fairy-tale statue of ice that shone more brightly than all the candles in the palace.

"It's magic," Stephen whispered.

As they came to the edge of the forest, they saw a humble cottage at the foot of the mountain. The king called a greeting. The man and his family came to the door and couldn't believe their eyes when they saw the two figures in the snow: the tall, powerful man with his load of logs and the small, slight boy with his sledge.

Once inside the cottage, the king coaxed the miserable fire in the hearth back to life. As Stephen unpacked the food and wine, the family slowly began to understand what was happening. Even so, Stephen could tell they hadn't realized who their visitor was – he certainly wasn't behaving like a king.

Soon there was a roaring fire, and the woman laid the table while the two youngest children sat on the king's knee. The eldest boy, who was about Stephen's age, looked wonderingly at him and gazed enviously at his hunting knife.

What a feast they had! Neither the children nor their parents had ever dreamed of such a spread. There was venison and roast pork, a plump goose, freshly baked bread, jellies and tarts, and an enormous spicy fruit custard. Soon they were all talking and laughing like old friends. Afterwards, when they all swore they couldn't eat another morsel, there was still enough left for a second feast the next day.

Stephen could have spent all night talking to the boy in front of the fire, but the king insisted they must go.

By the time they reached the edge of the forest, Stephen had made up his mind what to do. Swiftly he stole back to the cottage, felt for his precious hunting knife – and left it where the boy would be sure to see it in the morning. He knew the boy would treasure it even more than he did.

Then he ran back to join Wenceslas, guided by his own footprints. It was even colder now, but Stephen's heart was as warm as the king's as together they made their way back to the palace.

KING WENCESLAS
John Mason Neale (1818-1886)

Good King Wenceslas looked out, on the Feast of Stephen,
When the snow lay round about, deep and crisp and even.
Brightly shone the moon that night, though the frost was cruel,
When a poor man came in sight, gathering winter fuel.

"Hither, page, and stand by me, if thou knowst it, telling,
Yonder peasant, who is he, where and what his dwelling?"
"Sire, he lives a good league hence, underneath the mountain,
Right against the forest gate, by St Agnes' fountain."

"Bring me flesh and bring me wine, bring me pine logs hither,
Thou and I shalt see him dine, when we bear them thither."
Page and monarch forth they went, forth they went together,
Through the rude wind's wild lament and bitter weather.

"Sire, the night is darker now and the wind blows colder,
Fails my heart, I know not how, I can go no longer."
"Mark my footsteps, good my page, tread thou in them boldly,
Thou shalt find the winter's rage, freeze thy blood less coldly."

In his master's steps he trod, where the snow lay dinted.
Heat was in the very sod which the saint imprinted.
Therefore Christian men be sure, wealth or rank possessing,
Ye who now shalt bless the poor, shall yourselves find blessing.

The
Christmas Turkey
Meg Harper

Barney trudged up the lane from the bus stop. It was two weeks until Christmas and nearly dark. The lights from the farmhouse welcomed him. But there was something odd about the farm tonight. Barney puzzled over it with each tired step on the frost-hard ground. Something not quite right. Something…missing.

And then he knew. No! Not already! Not whilst he was out at school. She couldn't have. His tired legs span as he hurtled home. Through the gate. Past the silent pen. Across the yard. In at the kitchen door.

"Mum!" Barney stood on the doormat taking great, painful gulps of warm, kitchen air.

"Take your boots off, Barney," said his mother. She was peering at a casserole in the oven.

"Mum, the turkeys!"

"Now, don't start, Barney," said his mother. "You knew they had to go. It's nearly Christmas."

"But you didn't tell me it would be today," Barney wailed. "I never said goodbye."

His mother slammed the oven door. "I said, *don't* start, Barney. D'you think I wanted a fuss at breakfast? You've lived on a farm for nine years. It's time you got used to a few facts of life."

Barney stayed on the mat. He was trying hard not to cry. "Couldn't we have kept just one?" he mumbled.

"And what would you do with an ugly great turkey, might I ask? Take it for walks? Now get your boots off and come away from the door. You look half frozen."

"No thanks," said Barney and stalked back into the yard. This time it was going to be war. She never let him keep anything.

"What d'you want with a pet?" she'd say. "You'd only cry when it got old and died. You've a whole farm full of animals you can fuss over."

"But none of them is mine – not my very own."

"There's Fliss. You could take a bit more notice of her. She'd love to go for a romp in the fields with you. I never have the time."

"Fliss was Dad's dog." Always the same old argument.

"What about the cats then? They don't belong to anyone in particular."

Barney would try again. "I want something that's specially for me."

"Sounds like you're a bit too fussy for your own good," his mum would sniff. "Hundreds of kids would love to swap places with you – and you just turn your nose up!

You remember it's our animals that put food in your tummy and let's have less of this *me, me, me* business."

This time he'd had enough. One measly turkey wouldn't have cost anything. He could have fed it on scraps. And who was she to call turkeys ugly? She wasn't exactly an oil painting herself.

Hunger drew Barney back to the farmhouse. Fliss came up and licked him as he pulled at his boots. His mother was banging pans around. Uncle Ned was laying the table. A glorious aroma smacked Barney in the face as his mother lifted the casserole lid.

"Rabbit," said Barney's mother, curtly. "Your favourite."

Barney gulped. His mouth was watering already. "I'm not hungry," he said firmly, and then dropped his eyes as the grown-ups stared at him.

His mum spoke sharply. "If this is some tomfool protest about turkeys, it can stop now! There's good food in this pot and you need to eat it. I've never heard such nonsense. You'll not bring them back by starving."

"I told you, I'm not hungry," said Barney, hoping they couldn't hear his tummy rumbling.

He watched the colour mount in his mother's face. Any moment now she was going to yell. He braced himself.

Uncle Ned reached for the potatoes. "Best leave it, Pam," he said quietly, and began to help himself.

"Suit yourself," said Barney's mum stiffly, and she sat down.

By morning, Barney had dug himself in. "I've become a vegetarian," he announced, as he started on his third bowl of cornflakes. There was a long day ahead and probably no tea at the end of it.

"Don't be ridiculous, Barney," his mother snapped. "This is a FARM. We keep livestock. You've eaten meat all your life. It won't change anything if you stop now. The turkeys have gone to market and so will everything else."

"I don't care," stormed Barney, slamming down his spoon so hard that the milk leaped from his bowl. "I'm fed up of eating my FRIENDS!"

His mother paused. She had been making his peanut-butter sandwiches for school. "Now that's exactly what I mean," she said, in what was meant to be a patient voice. "If you're going to get all upset like this just because the turkeys have gone, what on earth would you be like if I let you have something as special as a pet? It'd have to go to market in the end."

"Why?" shouted Barney. "Why should it? Other kids have pets that they *keep*!"

"Other kids don't have mums struggling to make ends meet on tiny farms with only an old man to help!"

"But a turkey would hardly cost anything to keep. Not if it wasn't being fattened up for Christmas."

His mother tossed her head. "A turkey, is it? Now you're having me on. No child has ever wanted a turkey for a pet."

"I do," said Barney obstinately, and he stumped off to find his school bag.

After a week, Barney felt like surrendering. Surely they didn't normally have meat every night? Surely his mum cooked pizzas or macaroni cheese sometimes. But for a whole week Barney hadn't had any tea. There had been boiled ham and toad-in-the-hole and beefburgers and chicken drumsticks – it had gone on and on. Barney nearly gave in on the beefburgers night. He hadn't really thought about all the things he was going to miss. Then he remembered the turkeys. He remembered their gentle chuntering and their raucous, hysterical gobbling when he had stopped by their pen each evening. He remembered the comical way they tilted their heads and regarded him with their beady eyes. And he thought about them stripped and plucked and gleamingly golden for Christmas dinner. The war was still on.

On the tenth day – it was shepherd's pie for tea – Barney couldn't cope any longer. The school bus had been late and he had burned off all his energy shivering at the bus stop.

"Please," he said, hovering by the laden table. "Please could I have a cheese sandwich?"

"Bread's in the bread bin, cheese is in the fridge," said his mother, and she forked up a large mouthful of pie.

Barney found the bread knife and began to hack at the bread. Tears blurred his eyes. He hated it being like this. But he wasn't going to give in completely. Suddenly, the knife was taken from his hand.

"Easy does it, lad," said Uncle Ned. "You'll cut yourself, going on like that."

Barney watched as Uncle Ned cut four chunky slices, buttered them and spread them with thick layers of cheese. His mum kept her eyes on her shepherd's pie.

When Barney sauntered down for breakfast next day, his mother was hanging up Christmas decorations. The holidays had begun. Barney normally enjoyed helping with the Christmas preparations, but this year he hadn't the heart.

"Tell me something, Barney," said his mum, pausing

with tinsel in her hand. "What are you going to eat for Christmas dinner?"

Barney shrugged. "A cheese sandwich, I suppose."

She climbed down from the chair she was standing on and came close to him. "How long is this going to go on, Barney? D'you really think I'll let you become a vegetarian? You're only nine years old."

"Don't see why that makes any difference," said Barney, sulkily. "You don't have to be right, just because you're old."

"But what do you want me to do? Sell the farm and work in a factory? Cook special meals for you when I'm cooking meat for Ned and me?"

"We don't have meat that often," argued Barney. "Or we never used to. I could have a boiled egg or cheese on toast – I wouldn't starve."

"Oh yes, boiled eggs and cheese on toast! A fine healthy diet for a growing boy! Haven't I got enough worries without you going on this stupid hunger strike?"

Barney sighed. He had thought he was going to get through to her for a moment.

"Oh, eat your breakfast and get out of my way!" his mother snapped. "Can't you see I'm busy enough, without standing here arguing with you?"

Later, Barney sauntered into the yard. Uncle Ned was working on the gate of the old turkey pen. Barney wandered over and looked sadly at the empty space.

"She won't believe that I like turkeys," he said, quietly.

Uncle Ned grunted. He was old – a great uncle really – and never said very much. "Don't be too hard on her, Barney," he said. "She's a bit sensitive."

"But why?" grumbled Barney. "I only want a turkey – and to stop eating meat."

Uncle Ned gave Barney a very serious look. "And I always took you for a bright lad."

"But I don't understand," said Barney. For some unfathomable reason he felt like crying.

Uncle Ned rested a hand on his shoulder. "The farm

is all she lives for — and you, of course. She's pulling out all the stops, trying to keep it all together on her own — and there's you giving her a hard time about the turkeys!"

"Oh," said Barney, in a small voice. "I see. Well, I think I see." He sighed. Grown-ups were very complicated sometimes. "So why doesn't she want me to have a turkey of my own?" he asked, frowning.

"I guess because she doesn't want you hurt the way she's hurting now — and has been for the last three years."

Barney's eyes began to prickle. "But a turkey wouldn't just die," he said. "They live a good long time."

"I guess that's what we all thought about your dad," said Uncle Ned, gently.

"I can't remember Dad properly any more," said Barney, sniffing hard. "I wish he was still here."

"So does your mum," said Uncle Ned.

Barney marched back into the house. Fliss met him at the door and he fondled her head for a moment. His mum was rolling out pastry.

"Mum," he said, before he had time to think about it. "I'm sorry."

"That's all right, Barney," she said, a little stiffly.

"I'm not giving up though." He waited.

"No," she said, adjusting the pastry. "You take after your father."

Barney shook his head. "No," he said. "I take after you."

She looked at him in a way he had never seen before. For a fraction of a second she stroked his cheek with a floury finger. "No, I don't think so," she said, gently. "Now, you help me with these mince pies. It's vegetarian mincemeat."

That night she made his cheese sandwiches for him.

On Christmas morning, Barney woke up to find a satsuma in his stocking and an envelope with "From Father Christmas" printed across the front. He tore it open. "Your present is in the sheep shed," he read. Barney pulled on his clothes anyhow, clattered down the stairs and raced across the yard. It was cosy in the sheep shed – a few sheep had already been brought in for lambing. But in one of the pens, something strutted which wasn't a sheep at all. It was probably the ugliest young bird imaginable. But to Barney, it was beautiful. A Christmas turkey. His very own.

"Thank you, Mum," he breathed quietly, reaching out to touch the strange little creature, which chuntered in alarm. "Thank you."

And for Christmas dinner, he had macaroni cheese.

Holly and Ivy and Bah Humbug

Karen McCombie

"Andrea! There's a funny-looking dog rummaging in the bin bag outside!"

I frown in the direction of my dad, who has just yelled at my mum (Andrea) while I'm on the phone, about ten centimetres away from him. Annoyingly, my dad doesn't notice that a) I'm on the phone, or b) I'm frowning at him.

"What's the big deal?" I hear Mum calling down from

the spare room, where she's unpacking the Christmas decorations to put on the tree we're all going out to buy this Saturday morning. "It'll be Mrs. King's dog. She always lets it wander about on its own."

"Nah – it's not Elvis!" Dad bellows back, acting like Mum is on another continent, instead of just on another floor of our house. "This one's kind of scruffy-looking and white – you can hardly see it against the snow."

"*Dad*! I'm on the *phone*!" I spell it out to him, but he just grins and mouths "Bah Humbug!" at me and carries on stomping up the stairs so he can yak on to Mum about some unimportant dog minding its own business and chewing on a bin bag or whatever.

But anyway, Dad's not the only one who's bugging me while I'm trying to have a conversation.

"Lemme speak to her! Can I speak to Auntie Judy? Please, please, *please*, Holly?"

That's my little sister, Ivy. Just like always, she isn't waiting for me to answer her – she's just trying to grab the

phone while I'm talking. All I can do to stop her (without resorting to thumping her, which I'm *very* tempted to do sometimes, no matter how cute and adorable Mum and Dad think she is) is to keep swivelling around so she can't reach the receiver.

"Hey, Holly, have you thought of a present you'd like yet?" says the voice in my ear, unaware that I'm struggling to carry on this chat uninterrupted. "You know how I like to get some hints, so I don't get you something you'll hate!"

The voice in my ear belongs to my Auntie Judy. She's calling from the Isle of Mull, which is in Scotland. (Actually, being an island, it's not so much *in* Scotland as floating alongside of it.) I don't get to see Auntie Judy too often, since she lives a very *looooonnnnnnnggggg* train journey, a very bumpy ferry crossing and a car journey away from us, but I really like her. Except at this time of year, when she says insensitive stuff like, "Have you thought of a present you'd like yet, Holly?"

The problem I have is with the word "present". I don't want a "present"; I want "presents" – two to be exact. Don't go thinking I'm being horrible and greedy; it's just that it's not fair, having your birthday two days after Christmas. Everyone – including Auntie Judy and my grandparents and my mum and dad – has this INFURIATING habit of buying me a "joint" present, to cover Christmas *and* my birthday. Or buying me a "big" gift for Christmas, and then getting me just "little", "fun" and "extra" prezzies for my birthday. But it's not fair, is it? My best mate, Saskia, doesn't get a "big" present at Christmas and then just some bath bombs and a new pencil case for her birthday in June, does she? But that's what happens to me, just 'cause I have the bad luck to be born on the 27th of December.

"Well, I s'pose I would kind of like—"

Maybe I'm sounding a bit half-hearted when I try to answer Auntie Judy's question (not surprisingly), but I wouldn't mind getting the chance to *finish* the sentence. Unfortunately, Ivy has other ideas, and bounces like a

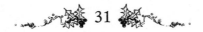

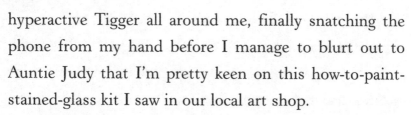

hyperactive Tigger all around me, finally snatching the phone from my hand before I manage to blurt out to Auntie Judy that I'm pretty keen on this how-to-paint-stained-glass kit I saw in our local art shop.

"Auntie Judy! It's *me*! It's Ivy!" my sister gabbles, keeping up the bouncing routine, like she's most definitely Tigger and not a six-just-about-to-go-on-seven-year-old girl.

She's bouncing 'cause she thinks it's cute and adorable, and that I'll be so overwhelmed by how cute and adorable she is (ha!) that I won't make a fuss and try to yank the phone back from her. But the thing is, I can't be bothered. I know I sound horribly grumpy, but for eleven-and-a-half months out of twelve I really am a bright and happy person (except when Ivy is winding me up, of course); it's just that this whole Christmas/birthday thing gets me ratty, and it doesn't help that Dad's nicknamed me "Bah Humbug" – after some Christmas-hating party-pooper in this ancient old story he's into – just 'cause he

can see I've gone a bit ratty.

And if some dumb nickname isn't bad enough, there's also the fact that I get teased something rotten about my stupid *real* name at this particular time of the year...

Oh yes. Since I'm in a moaning mood (sorry), let me moan a bit about being called Holly. I got named "Holly" because I was born at Christmas time. Maybe that sounds sort of cute and okay, if only my sister hadn't been born exactly *three years and one day* after me, and Mum and Dad hadn't decided to get all inspired by the festive season again and call her Ivy. So we're Holly and Ivy, just like the Christmas carol. It's so wet and corny, as the kids in my class just LOVE to remind me when Christmas rolls round.

"Ha ha ha!" Darren Sharp laughed at me yesterday. "Why didn't your parents just call you and your sister 'Santa' and 'Claus'? Or 'Snow' and 'Flake'?"

"Yeah? And why didn't yours just call you 'Dork'?" I suggested to him, feeling my face flush holly-berry red with rage.

Still, only my name and my birthday are to blame for irritating me at Christmas. The one thing that can irritate me the whole year round is bouncing around the hall about a metre away from me. Why, why, *why* did I end up with someone as annoying as Ivy for a sister? You're going to think I'm being mean and grouchy again, but seriously, all me and my sister have got in common is a) the same parents, b) lousy festive names, and c) the fact that our birthdays are so close to Christmas. Otherwise, we can't stand each other. The TV programmes I like, she yawns at. The pop stars she likes, I think are more dorky than Darren Sharp. Every time I try and talk to Mum and Dad, she bounces, bounds and yabbers away, so they get all starry-eyed and charmed and pay attention to her instead of me. Every time she tries to talk to Mum and Dad, I can't help yawning, 'cause whatever she yabbers on about is so dull and stupid I need coat hangers hooked under my eyelids to keep me from falling asleep.

"Um...I dunno," I hear Ivy say to Auntie Judy, finally

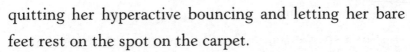

quitting her hyperactive bouncing and letting her bare feet rest on the spot on the carpet.

Whether Ivy still half expects me to grab the phone back or not, I don't care – I've lost interest, and find myself wandering over to the kitchen windowsill and staring out.

At a dog, as it happens.

And Dad is right – it's *not* Mrs. King's Elvis. Elvis is fat and shiny and black-furred, but this dog is different. Its fur is white and dull and goes in all directions, as if it's been brushed by a madman, or never been brushed for weeks at all. Narrowing my eyes, I decide that it can't have been brushed – or fed – for a long time, from the scruffy way it looks and the frantic licking going on with that empty tuna tin it's dragged from the bin bag.

"What are you looking at?" Ivy's irritating voice pipes up right beside me. Has she finished her conversation with Auntie Judy already? It was hardly worth her making such a fuss about grabbing the phone from me in the first place.

"A dog," I tell her flatly, keeping my eyes fixed on the snuffling stray outside. And I'm suddenly sure it *is* a stray – it couldn't look less loved than if it was dumped in a bin bag itself.

"Awww! It's cute!"

It's not often Ivy says something I agree with (usually when she speaks she comes out with something so loud and irritating that I wish I carried earplugs around with me). But she's right – it *is* a cute dog. It's staring up at us right now with the soppiest honey-brown eyes I've ever seen, all guilty and sad and lonely at the same time.

"Let's go out and pat it," Ivy announces, ready to haul the back door open and bounce outside, even if her feet are bare and there's a whole heap of snow on the path.

"Hold it! Not so loud. It's nervous and you'll scare it away," I tell her. "Go and put your shoes on while I get something for it to eat."

For a few seconds, we both silently bustle about; Ivy pulling on her new winter boots, and me rifling through the fridge and finding some smoked turkey that Dad likes for his sandwiches.

"It's still there, Holly," Ivy mumbles, standing on tiptoes in her red, suede boots, and squashing her nose on the glass panel of the back door. "Can we go and pat it now?"

But 'cause *I'm* the big sister, I decide to be the one to reach across and slowly turn the door handle. It squeaks really badly and I don't trust Ivy not to yank it and squeak it so loudly that our scrawny visitor sprints off in alarm, sending the tuna tin spinning.

"Hello, baby," Ivy coos, wriggling through the gap practically before I've even got the door open.

I peer out, half expecting the dog to be backing away, but it's still hovering nervously by our overflowing bin.

"It's shivering!" Ivy says sorrowfully, and before I can tell her to be careful and go slowly in case it bites, she bounds over and wraps her arms around the neck of the startled dog.

Okay, so it hasn't bitten her — that's a good start. But

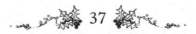

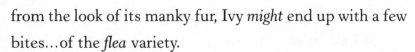

from the look of its manky fur, Ivy *might* end up with a few bites...of the *flea* variety.

"Hey doggy, want this?"

The dog flinches a little, as if it's more used to getting a smack from a hand coming its way, instead of the offer of some food. But one cautious sniff and it realizes its mistake and delicately snatches the cold meat from my hand, like it's worried I might change my mind and whisk it away.

"You're hungry, aren't you, doggy?" Ivy whispers, nudging its head with her nose (and probably picking up a few germs while she's at it). "It's a stray, isn't it, Hol? It's hungry and dirty and it doesn't have a collar."

"Maybe." I shrug vaguely, but I'm thinking exactly the same thing. "Hey, Ivy, let it go and see if I can get it to come over to the back door..."

Reluctantly, Ivy loosens her grip, as I walk backwards, holding out another turkey slice as bait. It's then that I spot a funny red mark on Ivy's skinny wrist, poking out

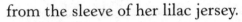

from the sleeve of her lilac jersey.

"What's that? On your arm?" I ask her, flipping my eyes from the red mark to the timidly following dog.

"Chinese burn," Ivy shrugs, taking baby steps alongside the dog and patting it reassuringly as it makes its wary way towards me and the back door.

"How come you got that?" I ask her, as another turkey slice gets gulped in one go.

"Got in a fight with Harry in my class," she explains.

"What about?"

I don't know Harry, or anyone else in Ivy's class apart from her best friend, Melina, who comes around for regular squealing and bouncing sessions at ours. But suddenly, I really, *really* don't like this boy I've never heard of.

"We did letters for Santa at school yesterday. No one was supposed to look, but Harry read what I'd asked for and told me I was stupid. I told him I wasn't, and then he hit me. So I thumped him back and then he gave me a Chinese burn. Then the teacher saw and told us both off for fighting."

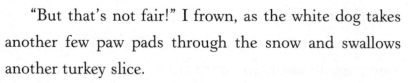

"But that's not fair!" I frown, as the white dog takes another few paw pads through the snow and swallows another turkey slice.

"I know," Ivy shrugs again, sounding very grown-up and matter-of-fact about the whole incident. "Hey, look – it's nearly there! Give it some more turkey, Holly!"

"Yeah, yeah, okay, Ivy," I tell her, stepping up onto the doorstep and unravelling another piece of meat from the plastic packet. "But what did that horrible kid think was so stupid about your Santa letter? What did you ask for?"

"A new birthday. And a new name."

Um...I guess I'd expected her to say a complete collection of Pop Idol videos, or a trampoline for extra bouncing, or some kind of doll's house for her stupid dolls or something. I hadn't expected her to want...well, what *I* wanted.

"But how come?" I ask her, looking at my kid sister in wonder.

"Well, I want a new birthday 'cause mine is too close

to Christmas and no one ever gives me two proper presents. Even Auntie Judy asked me what I wanted as a joint present just now on the phone," says Ivy, twining her fingers into the white dog's fur. "And Ivy's a *stupid* name. Specially when I've got a sister called Holly. Harry and the other boys have been teasing me about it ever since we've been practising Christmas carols for the school concert."

Wow.

Wow that my sister has the same grudge against our birthdays and our names. I thought she hadn't noticed. I thought Ivy was always too busy bouncing and charming the pants off of everyone to care about stuff like that.

And wow that I've been so surprised by what Ivy has just said that I hadn't noticed that we've got all the way into the kitchen – me, Ivy and the white dog. Ivy is quietly closing the door and the dog is gazing around, sniffing the air for lingering Saturday morning breakfast smells. It still seems nervous, but – and I'm not exactly an expert on dogs – it looks kind of, well, *happy* to me.

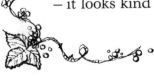

"Holly? Ivy? Are you two nearly ready?" We hear Dad's voice call out, as his footsteps begin thumping down the staircase. "Let's get shopping for that tree – and see if we can't find you two a great present each while we're at it!"

At the sound of Dad's cheery but gruff tone, the dog's honey-brown eyes flicker worriedly from my face to Ivy's, with one ear tilted up and the other flopping down pathetically.

"Don't worry. It's all right," I tell the dog, reaching out and ruffling the floppy ear.

"Holly!" Ivy hisses at me urgently, as Dad's footsteps thump down the last few stairs. "I don't care about present shopping! Can't we ask to keep the dog? Like a special Christmas and birthday present all rolled into one – for both of us?"

The dog gazes up at me pleadingly, same as Ivy does.

But neither of them need to plead. For only the second time ever, I totally agree with my annoying little

sister. I don't care about a new pair of trainers or a CD player or a stained glass art set. I want this scruffy white dog. And I know it won't be easy – first we'll have to convince Mum and Dad that it's a great idea, then we'll have to do the right thing and check with the police that no one has reported a missing white dog (and I bet six mince pies and a Christmas pudding that no one *will* have, the state it's in).

"It's a deal!" I smile at Ivy and the dog.

Ivy seems about to smile back, when she catches sight of our dad, standing stock still in the kitchen doorway.

Immediately, she goes into fully bouncy, cute, adorable mode, and for once it doesn't bug me.

"Look, Dad!" Ivy trills, jumping up and doing her best Tigger impersonation, startling the white dog while she's at it. "It's a puppy! Do you think it's for us? Or is it an early birthday prezzie from you and Mum, for me and Holly?"

I'm the big sister, but suddenly Ivy's in charge, and

when she zaps me a quick sideways glance to help her out, I do my best.

"It's really friendly, Dad," I chip in, throwing my arm around the dog (it's definitely a grown-up dog and *not* a puppy). "And we've thought of a name for it already – it's called...it's called...Bah Humbug! Humbug for short!"

The scruffy white dog pants happily, as though living here and being called Humbug is the best news it's heard in a *long* time. Or maybe it's just panting at the last slice of turkey it's spotted me holding in my other hand.

"Er, Andrea..." Dad shouts over his shoulder, a grin a mile wide spreading across his face. "There's a funny-looking dog in our kitchen now!"

"*What?!*" we hear Mum squawk from upstairs.

But squawks or not, that grin of Dad's tells me and Ivy and Bah Humbug that this *might* just be the *best* Christmas/birthday present any of us has ever had.

Though maybe we'll need to ask Santa to bring us a can of flea spray...

ROOM AT THE INN

Helena Pielichaty

Nazareth

Bethlehem

Spittal-in-the-Wold Primary School
December 2nd

Mrs. Ellison tilted her chin and waited for silence. It came at once from the fifteen juniors in front of her. She hadn't taught in the village school for over thirty years without knowing how to command instant attention, even when wearing Rudolph the red-nosed reindeer earrings. "Right,

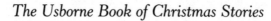

mateys. We've got two weeks before the end of term. The classroom is looking fantastic..." she paused and allowed everyone to survey the morning's handiwork once again.

The classroom did look cracking, ten-year-old Lucas Whittaker reckoned. Really festive. The long, narrow windows had been sprayed so thoroughly with fake snow that there was hardly any glass left to see through, and the Christmas mobiles hanging from the rafters sparkled as the ceiling lights reflected from each glued creation of baubles, tinsel and toilet rolls.

Lucas was particularly proud of the "grotto" area, which he and Stephen Clay and Winnie Scothern had assembled in the book corner. It even had a disabled access, bordered with red and green tree lights, which flashed along either side of the ramp when Stephen manoeuvred up it in his wheelchair.

"...that just leaves the Nativity to rehearse," Mrs. Ellison announced.

Stephen Clay groaned. He couldn't think of anything

more boring, but Lucas sat up straight. He loved drama, and longed for a speaking role. He knew he was in with a chance this year. Mrs. Ellison always chose the older ones for the main roles and as there was only one Year Six in the school, the Year Fives had to be in pole position.

"Right," Mrs. Ellison said, rustling the much-used scripts before glancing round, "first of all, the parts..."

Stephen raised his hand.

"Yes, Stephen?"

"Can I be Mary?" he volunteered, thinking it would be a right laugh if she let him.

"No, you can't be Mary," Mrs. Ellison said, firmly.

"Why not?"

The teacher's earrings dangled impatiently. "You know very well why not! The Nativity isn't a pantomime. Nobody shouted, 'He's behind you!' to Mary when Gabriel appeared, did they?"

"Pity," Stephen said.

Mrs. Ellison frowned. "Well, they didn't. Just

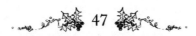

remember, the Nativity is the real reason we have Christmas at all. I want serious actors for serious roles."

Serious actors for serious roles! "That's me," thought Lucas, sitting up even straighter, his heart pounding in his chest.

Whittaker's Farm, two miles up the road
4.10pm

Mrs. Whittaker gasped at the sound of Noodle, their collie, barking like mad. The excited tone of the barks could only mean one thing – Lucas was home already. Crumbs! It didn't seem two minutes since she'd packed him off to school this morning. Where did the time go? Since opening the farm for bed and breakfast last summer she never seemed to get ahead of herself. To think it was Christmas in three weeks – *three weeks* – unbelievable! After pushing a strand of loose, brown hair back behind her ear, she slammed the washing-machine door shut and

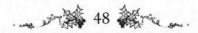

stepped into the kitchen to greet her son. She had to share some awkward news with him and she needed to gauge his mood. "How was your day?" she asked, brightly.

Lucas shrugged off his school bag and unfastened his coat. "It was good. We finished the grotto and Mrs. Ellison gave us our par—"

But before Lucas could continue, they were interrupted by the arrival of Mr. Freshney, the lodger here on an extended stay to research the history of the Dambusters. Lucas sighed, trying not to mind the interruption. He was kind of used to it from this particular guest.

The man had a frown on his face deeper than a quarry as he held out the bale of fresh, peachy coloured towels from his room. "Ah! Mrs. Whittaker – not keen on pastels. Prefer white. Mind if you exchange them?" he asked in that short, clipped way he had.

Mrs. Whittaker immediately took the offending items. "Not a problem, Mr. Freshney. Lucas, run upstairs and put some white towels in Mr. Freshney's room, there's a good lad."

Lucas did as he was told, passing the man on the stairs on the way back down. Mr. Freshney looked straight through him. "Don't say thank you then," Lucas thought.

Back in the kitchen, Mrs. Whittaker was preparing him a snack of ginger biscuits and apple. "You were telling me about school," she prompted.

"Oh yeah," Lucas said, taking a biscuit and biting it in half. "I'm in the Nativity. I'm the innkeeper."

"That's nice."

"I only get one weedy line though," he said, trying to hide his disappointment. He couldn't believe Mrs. Ellison had given the part of Joseph to Stephen after how cheeky he'd been. He reached for a chunk of apple and sighed hard.

"I've got something to tell you, too," Lucas's mother said, not quite meeting his eyes. "You know next weekend, when it's the Christmas Market and we're fully booked?"

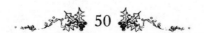

"Yes?"

"I've double-booked one of the rooms – don't ask me how – I just have."

"So?" asked Lucas, reaching across for another biscuit. He was always starving straight after school, and a quick peek at the pan-free cooker told him there'd be no dinner for a while.

His mother threw him an apologetic glance. "You're going to have to go up in the loft – just for two nights. I need to use your room."

Lucas scowled, thinking of the cramped loft space that smelled of pickled onions, and the floorboards that creaked even when nothing was there. "Can't they just go to another B & B?"

"Well, I've tried phoning round, but everywhere is full. Besides, the extra money will be really useful, especially so near Christmas." She looked at him pleadingly. "It's only for two nights," she repeated.

"Whatever," Lucas mumbled.

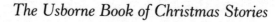

Spittal-in-the-Wold Primary School
December 3rd
First Rehearsal

Lucas's stomach clenched as Joseph and Mary approached. He crouched behind the cardboard door of the grotto, which had now become the inn, waiting for the knock, and duly delivered his line when Stephen asked him if there was any room. "I am sorry we are full. I do have a stable you could use, though," he said in a loud, clear voice.

Stephen, not choosing quite the same words as those written for him, grinned. "Result! Cheers pal," he said, and continued on his way. Lucas stared after him, a thoughtful look on his face.

Whittaker's Farm
9.10pm

It was past bedtime, but Lucas had pleaded the homework

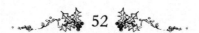

excuse so he didn't have to go upstairs just yet. It was so
cosy in the living room with the log fire burning, and Dad
reading the Echo in one chair and Mum writing
Christmas cards in another. Besides, even if he did go to
bed, Lucas knew he wouldn't get to sleep because Mr.
Freshney always had his television on so loud he could
hear it in his bedroom two doors away.

"Have we got another Bible?" Lucas asked, scowling
at the one in his hand.

"Another Bible? Why?" Mr. Whittaker replied, without
looking up from the sports pages.

"This one's not detailed enough. I've read through
every Gospel: Matthew, Mark, Luke and John, and the
innkeeper only comes in to it once, in Luke, and even
that's a pretty feeble mention. There must be more in
another version."

Lucas's mother licked yet another envelope, screwing
her nose up at the taste. "Well, that's the same Bible they use
in chapel, ducky. I can't see it being any different from—"

53

The bell in the hallway cut her short. "That'll be you-know-who," she said, rising instantly from her chair. Lucas followed her with his eyes, wondering how she could stand it, always putting the guests first, day and night, no matter how troublesome they were.

"What was it this time?" Mr. Whittaker asked when she returned a few minutes later. "Not the radiator again?"

"The complimentary biscuits. He wanted custard creams instead of Bourbons."

Lucas's father laughed shortly and began the crossword. Lucas closed the Bible, more thoughtful than ever.

Spittal-in-the-Wold Primary School
December 10th
Fourth Rehearsal

Lucas was once more crouched behind the cardboard door.

"Excuse me sir, have you any room at the inn?"

Stephen asked politely, rubbing one finger up the side of his face in a rude gesture only Lucas saw.

Lucas repeated his line slowly. "I am sorry I am full but you could always..." he began, then hesitated as he caught Mrs. Ellison's eye, "...but I do have a stable you could use," he finished, lamely.

"Cool," Stephen replied, cheerfully.

As Joseph and Mary followed Lucas's outstretched arm and made their way towards the stable, Lucas felt himself growing confused and even annoyed. No innkeeper worth his salt would do this, he thought. No way. That Luke bloke was well out of order.

Whittaker's Farm
December 12th

It was late on the Saturday night of the busiest weekend of the Whittakers' bed-and-breakfasting career. People had been arriving all day, asking for hotter water, colder

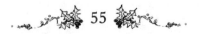

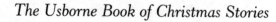

water, warmer rooms, cooler rooms, vegetarian breakfasts, spare hairdryers and tips on parking spots near the market. Up in the loft, Lucas had been glad to escape, and was listening to the cold wind howling outside as his mother arrived to kiss him goodnight.

"Mum?"

"That's me."

"If someone turned up on the doorstep now and they wanted a room, even though we're stuffed to the rafters, what would you do?"

"Shoot myself," she yawned.

"Seriously."

His mother rubbed her face tiredly. "I don't know – recommend somewhere else, I suppose."

"But everywhere's full – you said so – and what if it was much later on? You know, the middle of the night, and they were lost and really tired and desperate and the wife had a broken leg and their car had broken down and they looked kind."

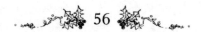

"Blinking heck – I don't know – sort something out for them, I guess. Therapy by the sound of it."

"You wouldn't shove them in the barn, would you?"

"No, of course not."

Lucas nodded. "That's what I thought."

Spittal-in-the-Wold Methodist Chapel
16th December
Dress Rehearsal

It was all going like clockwork, just as Mrs. Ellison liked things. Letters had been sent home about the Nativity Play, the programmes had been photocopied, the Minister was happy to say a few words in chapel afterwards, and the PTA were organizing party food for when they all returned to the school. Just one more run-through and the kids would be perfect, too. "Okay," Mrs. Ellison said to the assembled cast, twiddling her new snowman earrings, "the innkeeper's scene."

Stephen wheeled himself up the ramp, with the heavily cushioned Mary by his side. Everyone watched as the pair reached the cardboard door of the inn. Stephen leaned forward and knocked. Lucas appeared instantly, his long, bushy false beard bouncing on his chest. "Have you got a room free, sir?" Stephen asked the innkeeper politely. "Only my wife's heavy...with child."

"Very good, Stephen," Mrs. Ellison thought to herself. She had warned him not to mess about any more *or else*, after he'd tried to affix a "Caution, Baby on Board" sticker to the back of his wheelchair. He appeared to be taking notice. Relieved, she waited for Lucas to deliver his line.

"I am sorry, I am full," Mrs. Ellison mouthed when he seemed to be taking a long time about it. What was he fidgeting with under his robe?

"A room?" Lucas asked, his face full of doubt. "I'll just check for you," he said, unexpectedly producing his mother's spiral-bound diary, which she used for pencilling in bookings. He sighed deeply and shook his head. "It's

not looking good," he continued. "We're full to bursting but seeing as these are exceptional circumstances, you can have the kids' room. They won't mind bunking up with me and the wife for one night."

"You what?" asked a baffled Stephen Clay.

Lucas continued unabashed. "Breakfast's eight till ten – will you be wanting a full English or Continental?" He raised his eyebrows and waited for Stephen's response, knowing his mate wouldn't be able to resist departing from the script. He was right.

Totally forgetting Mrs. Ellison's warning, Stephen threw himself into the improvised dialogue. "Well, full English of course, pal, but hold the black pudding – it makes me trump," he replied, going over-the-top as usual.

"No problem. Come in," Lucas beckoned, ignoring everyone's giggles. "You're just in time for the news. That Herod, eh? What a nutter!"

"Tell me about it," replied Stephen, "I was just saying to Mary—"

 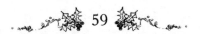

"Lucas Whittaker! Stephen Clay! What do you think you are doing?" Mrs. Ellison demanded angrily, her voice echoing as it bounced off the cold, white chapel walls.

Lucas turned to face the headteacher, his head held high. He was prepared for this.

Whittaker's Farm
4.00pm

"She wouldn't believe me," Lucas said, trying not to cry.

"What's that, ducky?" Mrs. Whittaker asked, fussing uncharacteristically round her pale-faced son, handing him a cup of sweetened tea and a mince pie.

Lucas pushed them miserably to the side. "Mrs. Ellison. I tried to tell her an innkeeper wouldn't turn away Joseph and Mary, 'specially when Mary was having a baby and after she'd just ridden for seventy miles on a bloomin' donkey. That's how far it is from Nazareth to Bethlehem you know – I looked it up."

"Oh, ducky," was all his mother could think of replying.

"Well, he wouldn't, would he? I think Luke got his facts muddled in the Bible and I told her so, too."

"Oh heck..."

"...because even if every room was used up, an innkeeper would find a space because guests always come first, don't they? I said to Mrs. Ellison, I said, look, if you don't believe me, come to our house. There's not one sign that it's nearly Christmas because nobody's had time to trim up or to bake any cakes or go Christmas shopping or anything. That's because we're too busy jumping to it for everyone else, even whinging, whining old—"

"Lucas!" his mother warned.

Her son wiped his eyes angrily. "Well, it's true and you know it. So what we'd do if a tired couple with a baby due any second turned up, I don't know. We definitely wouldn't shove 'em in the barn, would we? You said so yourself! More likely I'd end up in there with Noodle."

Mrs. Whittaker tried not to smile at the thought of

what Lucas would say if she did send him to the barn, where she had set aside two hours wrapping and hiding certain things for certain people not a hundred miles from where she was sitting. "So what did Mrs. Ellison say?" she asked, gently.

Lucas sighed with frustration. "She said she was glad I felt so strongly, but I couldn't go changing the course of history like that."

Mrs. Whittaker got up and gave her son a hug, folding her arms tightly round him. "Well, she does have a point. If Jesus had been born in a nice comfy bed, it wouldn't be the same story, would it?"

"I suppose."

"Think about it. He'd have nothing in common with the poor people who loved him then, would he? Like the shepherds and what have you."

"I suppose."

"But you're right, if Mary and Joseph had arrived here, we would have let them in, wouldn't we, no messing?"

 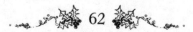

Lucas nodded, calming down and feeling better now that his mother agreed with him. "Yeah, we would. And I bet they wouldn't have cared if they got white towels or peachy, either."

"Never mind, eh? But you are still in the play aren't you?"

"Yes, I'm still in the play," he sniffed.

"Good."

"And I'm allowed to keep in the appointment diary. Mrs. Ellison said that was a nice touch," Lucas added, perking up a little more.

"That's good."

"But I mustn't let them in."

"No."

"Not even for a cup of tea and a biscuit."

"No. Best stick to the script."

"Yep," Lucas agreed, "best stick to the old, old script."

"Excuse me," said Mr. Freshney from the doorway, "about the shower in the *en suite...*"

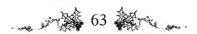

Stow-by-Spittal Methodist Chapel
December 18th
The Nativity Play

"The trouble with plays," Lucas thought, as he listened to the applause from the audience, "is they go too fast. You spend weeks rehearsing and it's over and done with in a flash, especially when you've only got one line to deliver."

"Well done, everybody," Mrs. Ellison beamed, clapping louder than anyone. "You were all brilliant. Brilliant!"

"Never mind that," Stephen Clay said as they filed into the back of the chapel, "where's the nosh?"

Afterwards, Mrs. Ellison had a quiet word with her innkeeper. "You all right, Lucas?" she asked him. "You're not still mad at me for being such a stickler to tradition?"

Lucas, tucking in to his fifth tuna roll, shook his head vigorously. "No, miss, you were right. It was the way it had to be. The story wouldn't have been the same if Jesus hadn't been born in the stable – I guess Luke was spot on, really."

"I think so too."

 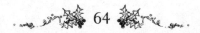

"Though I still reckon the innkeeper got a rough deal. One line's not much, considering," Lucas couldn't help adding.

His teacher smiled broadly. "Oh, but just remember, a good actor can say more in one line than a poor one can in ten."

"Really?"

"Really. You should know."

Lucas grinned, realizing she had paid him a huge compliment. "Thanks, miss."

She grinned back, the silver, star-shaped earrings the class had bought her twinkling as they caught the light. "Merry Christmas, Lucas."

"Merry Christmas, Mrs. Ellison."

The
Fairy Ship

Alison Uttley

Little Tom was the son of a sailor. He lived in a small white-washed cottage in Cornwall, on the rocky cliffs looking over the sea. From his bedroom window he could watch the great waves with their curling plumes of white foam, and count the seagulls as they circled in the blue sky. The water went right away to the dim horizon, and sometimes Tom could see the smoke from ships like a dark flag in the distance. Then he ran to get his spyglass, to get a better view.

Tom's father was somewhere out on that great stretch of ocean, and all Tom's thoughts were there, following him, wishing for him to come home. Every day he ran down the narrow path to the small rocky bay, and sat there waiting for the ship to return. It was no use to tell him that a ship could not enter the tiny cove with its sharp needles of rocks and dangerous crags. Tom was certain that he would see his sailor father step out to the strip of sand if he kept watch. It seemed the proper way to come home.

December brought wild winds that swept the coast. Little Tom was kept indoors, for the gales would have blown him away like a gull's feather if he had gone to the rocky pathway. He was deeply disappointed that he couldn't keep watch in his favourite place. A letter had come, saying that his father was on his way home and any time he might arrive. Tom feared he wouldn't be there to see him, and he stood by the window for hours watching the sky and the wild tossing sea.

"What shall I have for Christmas, Mother?" he asked one day. "Will Father Christmas remember to bring me something?"

"Perhaps he will, if our ship comes home in time," smiled his mother, and then she sighed and looked out at the wintry scene.

"Will he come in a sleigh with eight reindeer pulling it?" persisted Tom.

"Maybe he will," said his mother, but she wasn't thinking what she was saying. Tom knew at once, and he pulled her skirt.

"Mother! I don't think so. I don't think he will," said he.

"Will what, Tom? What are you talking about?"

"Father Christmas won't come in a sleigh, because there isn't any snow here. Besides, it is too rocky, and the reindeer would slip. I think he'll come in a ship, a grand ship with blue sails and a gold mast."

Little Tom took a deep breath and his eyes shone.

"Don't you think so, Mother? Blue sails, or maybe red

ones. Satin like our parlour cushion. My father will come back with him. He'll come in a ship full of presents, and Father Christmas will give him some for me."

Tom's mother suddenly laughed aloud.

"Of course he will, little Tom. Father Christmas comes in a sleigh drawn by a team of reindeer to the children of towns and villages, but to the children of the sea he sails in a ship with all the presents tucked away in the hold."

She took her little son up in her arms and kissed him, but he struggled away and went back to the window.

"I'm going to be a sailor soon," he announced proudly. "Soon I shall be big enough, and then I shall go over the sea."

He looked out at the stormy sea where his father was sailing, every day coming nearer home, and on that wild water he saw only mist and spray, and the cruel waves dashing over the jagged splinters of rock.

Christmas morning came, and it was a day of surprising

sunshine and calm. The seas must have known it was Christmas and they kept peace and goodwill. They danced into the cove in sparkling waves, and fluttered their flags of white foam, and tossed their treasures of seaweed and shells on the narrow beach.

Tom awoke early, and looked in his stocking on the bedpost. There was nothing in it at all! He wasn't surprised. Land children had their presents dropped down the chimney, but he, a sailor's son, had to wait for the ship. The stormy weather had kept the Christmas ship at sea, but now she was bound to come.

His mother's face was happy and excited, as if she had a secret. Her eyes shone with joy, and she seemed to dance round the room in excitement, but she said nothing.

Tom ate his breakfast quietly – a bantam egg and some honey for a special treat. Then he ran outside, to the gate, and down the slippery grassy path which led to the sea.

"Where are you going, Tom?" called his mother. "You wait here, and you'll see something."

"No, Mother. I'm going to look for the ship, the little Christmas ship," he answered, and away he trotted, so his mother turned to the house, and made her own preparations for the man she loved. The tide was out and it was safe now the winds had dropped.

She looked through the window, and she could see the little boy sitting on a rock on the sand, staring away at the sea. His gold hair was blown back, his blue jersey was wrinkled about his stout little body. The gulls swooped round him as he tossed scraps of bread to feed them. Jackdaws came whirling from the cliffs and a raven croaked hoarsely from its perch on a rocky peak.

The water was deep blue, like the sky, and purple shadows hovered over it, as the waves gently rocked the cormorants fishing there. The little boy leaned back in his sheltered spot, and the sound of the water made him drowsy. The sweet air lulled him and his head began to droop.

Then he saw a light so beautiful he had to rub his eyes

to get the sleep out of them. The wintry sun made a pathway on the water, flickering with points of light on the crests of the waves, and down this golden lane came a tiny ship that seemed no larger than a toy. She moved swiftly through the water, making for the cove, and Tom cried out with joy and clapped his hands as she approached.

The wind filled the blue satin sails, and the sunbeams caught the mast of gold. On deck was a company of sailors dressed in white, and they were making music of some kind, for shrill squeaks and whistles and pipings came through the air. Tom leaned forward to watch them, and as the ship came nearer he could see that the little sailors were playing flutes, tootling a hornpipe, then whistling a carol.

He stared very hard at their pointed faces, and little pink ears. They were not sailor-men at all, but a crew of white mice! There were four-and-twenty of them – yes, twenty-four white mice with gold rings round their snowy necks, and gold rings in their ears!

The little ship sailed into the cove, through the barriers of sharp rocks, and the white mice hurried backwards and forwards, hauling at the silken ropes, casting the gold anchor, crying with high voices as the ship came to port close to the rock where Tom sat waiting and watching.

Out came the Captain – and would you believe it? He was a Duck, with a cocked hat like Nelson's, and a blue jacket trimmed with gold braid. Tom knew at once he was Captain Duck because under his wing he carried a brass telescope, and by his side was a tiny sword.

He stepped boldly down the gangway and waddled to the eager little boy.

"Quack! Quack!" said the Captain, saluting Tom, and Tom of course stood up and saluted back.

"The ship's cargo is ready, Sir," said the Duck. "We have sailed across the sea to wish you a merry Christmas. You will find everything in order, Sir. My men will bring the merchandise ashore, and here is the Bill of Lading."

The Duck held out a piece of seaweed, and Tom took it. "Thank you, Captain Duck," said he. "I'm not a very good reader yet, but I can count up to twenty-four."

"Quack! Quack!" cried the Duck, saluting again. "Quick! Quick!" he said, turning to the ship, and the four-and-twenty white mice scurried down to the cabin and dived into the hold.

Then up on deck they came, staggering under their burdens, dragging small bales of provisions, little oaken casks, baskets, sacks and hampers. They raced down the ship's ladders, and clambered over the sides, and swarmed down the gangway. They brought their packages ashore and laid them on the smooth sand near Tom's feet.

There were almonds and raisins, bursting from silken sacks. There were sugarplums and goodies, pouring out of wicker baskets. There was a host of tiny toys, drums and marbles, tops and balls, pearly shells, and a flying kite, a singing bird and a musical box.

When the last toy had been safely carried from the ship

the white mice scampered back. They weighed anchor, singing "Yo-heave-ho!" and they ran up the rigging. The Captain cried "Quack! Quack!" and he stood on the ship's bridge. Before Tom could say "Thank you", the little golden ship began to sail away, with flags flying, and the blue satin sails tugging at the silken cords. The four-and-twenty white mice waved their sailor hats to Tom, and the Captain looked at him through his spyglass.

Away went the ship, swift as the wind, a glittering speck on the waves. Away she went towards the far horizon along that bright path that the sun makes when it shines on water.

Tom waited till he could see her no more, and then he stooped over his presents. He tasted the almonds and raisins, he sucked the goodies, he beat the drum, and tinkled the musical box and the iron triangle. He flew the kite, and tossed the balls in the air, and listened to the song of the singing-bird. He was so busy playing that he did not hear soft footsteps behind him.

Suddenly he was lifted up in a pair of strong arms and pressed against a thick blue coat, and two bright eyes were smiling at him.

"Well, Thomas, my son! Here I am! You didn't expect me, now did you? A Happy Christmas, Tom, boy. I crept down soft as a snail, and you never heard a tinkle of me, did you?"

"Oh, Father!" Tom flung his arms round his father's neck and kissed him many times. "Oh, Father. I knew you were coming. Look! They've been, they came just before you, in the ship."

"Who, Tom? Who's been? I caught you fast asleep. Come along home and see what Father Christmas has brought you. He came along o' me, in my ship, you know. He gave me some presents for you."

"He's been here already, just now, in a little gold ship, Father," cried Tom, stammering with excitement. "He's just sailed away. He was a Duck, Captain Duck, and there were four-and-twenty white mice with him. He left me all these toys. Lots of toys and things."

Tom struggled to the ground, and pointed to the sand, but where the treasure of the fairy ship had been stored there was only a heap of pretty shells and seaweed and striped pebbles. "They's all gone," he cried, choking back a sob, but his father laughed and carried him off, pick-a-back, up the narrow footpath to the cottage.

"You've been dreaming, my son," said he. "Father Christmas came with me, and he's brought you a fine lot of toys, and I've got them at home for you."

"Didn't dream," insisted Tom. "I saw them all."

On the table in the kitchen lay such a medley of presents that Tom opened his eyes wider than ever. There were almonds and raisins, and goodies in little coloured sacks, and a musical box with a picture of a ship on its round lid. There was a drum with scarlet edges, and a book, and a pearly shell from a far island, and a kite of thin paper from China, and a love-bird in a cage. Best of all there was a little model of his father's ship, which his father had carved for Tom.

"Why, these are like the toys from the fairy ship," cried Tom. "Those were very little ones, like fairy toys, and these are big ones, real ones."

"Then it must have been a dream-ship," said his mother. "You must tell us all about it."

So little Tom told the tale of the ship with blue satin sails and gold mast, and he told of the four-and-twenty white mice with gold rings round their necks, and the Captain Duck, who said "Quack! Quack!" His father sat listening, as the words came tumbling from the excited little boy.

When Tom had finished, the sailor said, "I'll sing you a song of that fairy-ship, our Tom. Then you'll never forget what you saw."

He waited a moment, gazing into the great fire on the hearth, and then he stood up and sang this song to his son and to his wife.

The Fairy Ship

There was a ship a-sailing,
A-sailing on the sea.
And it was deeply laden,
With pretty things for me.

There were raisins in the cabin,
And almonds in the hold,
The sails were made of satin,
And the mast it was of gold.

The four-and-twenty sailors
That stood between the decks
Were four-and-twenty white mice
With rings about their necks.

The Captain was a Duck, a Duck,
With a jacket on his back,
And when this fairy-ship set sail,
The Captain he said "Quack".

"Oh, sing it again," cried Tom, clapping his hands, and his father sang once more the song that later became a nursery rhyme.

It was such a lovely song that Tom hummed it all that happy Christmas Day, and it just fitted into the tune on his musical box. He sang it to his children when they were little, long years later, and you can sing it too if you like!

The Day Rosaleen Stole Baby Jesus

Martin Waddell

This story is about me, Eileen O'Hare, and my brother Mickey and the mess our wee sister, Rosaleen, got us into over the school Christmas crib.

I'm ten. Mickey is nine. Our Rosaleen is five and she has just started in Miss O'Neill's Reception Class. We take turns seeing her safe home after school, which is no small order, for she is always getting into trouble one way or another.

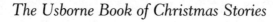

It was one of Mickey's days for kicking a football about with the two Gormans, snow or no snow, so there I was on Rosaleen duty, plodding up Harbour Lane past the church to our house, with Rosaleen behind me. She was looking kind of lumpy round the middle, walking slowly. She'd had her winter coat on and buttoned when I came to collect her from the wee ones' room, and that's not like her. Usually I'm stuck with doing her buttons up, for it takes her all day to do them.

"You've something bumpy hid up your coat!" I told her. "Open up then!"

She did...reluctantly.

The bumpy bit under her coat turned out to be the Baby Jesus, from our school crib.

"You stole Baby Jesus!" I said slowly.

Nobody ever-ever-*ever* stole the Baby Jesus from the crib in the whole history of our school, but our Rosaleen had just done it, which was absolutely typical. I did the only thing I could do. I turned her right round and ran

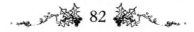

back down Harbour Lane to our school, so we could put Baby Jesus back before anyone knew he'd been away on his holidays.

The school was all shut up when we got there.

"This time you've really done it!" I said sharply, for I knew there'd be a terrible row about it.

"It wasn't me, our Eileen," Rosaleen said anxiously, and her lip started to quiver.

"If it wasn't you stuck the Baby Jesus up your coat, then who was it?" was what I was thinking, but I know from long experience how Rosaleen's funny wee mind works. "*What* wasn't you?" I asked, trying to be patient, and work the story out of her. We'd get round to the *why* of it her way, and standing there scolding her in the playground wasn't going to help.

"It wasn't me knocked into our crib and broke Mary and Joseph," she burst out, all in a rush. "It was Sean Logan. Sean Logan was crying because he thought Mrs. O'Regan would kill him. Miss O'Neill said it would be all

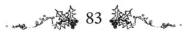

right and what Mrs. O'Regan didn't know about would never hurt her. Miss O'Neill's taken Mary and Joseph home with her to fix them with glue."

That sounded right. Miss O'Neill is a soft touch when it comes to her babies in Reception Class. I could just see her telling Sean Logan she'd fix things without our headteacher, the Rocket O'Regan, finding out. What I couldn't figure out was how that added up to Baby Jesus coming home under our Rosaleen's coat.

"A baby like that needs his mammy and daddy to look after him," Rosaleen explained patiently, as if I ought to know that and she had to spell it out for me.

"So?" I said. "We don't have a mammy and daddy for him."

"So there's the *other* ones," she said. "The big Mary and big Joseph, in the big crib at our church."

"The big Mary and Joseph have a big Baby Jesus of their own," I told her.

"It's all the *same* Baby Jesus to them," she replied. "I

84

promised Baby Jesus I'd take him to see the big Mary and the big Joseph and the donkey in church and I'd look after him at our house till Miss O'Neill glued his *other* mammy and daddy."

There she was, with tears threatening, and as usual she'd *meant* well...but I was going to get into a whole cartload of bother if anyone found out what she'd done.

"Wasn't it a grand idea?" she went on, hopefully. "Wee Baby Jesus would have been lonely all night in the dark school with no mammy and daddy, so I promised him he wouldn't be."

"Stop her tears before they get going," I thought. Rosaleen arriving home tear-stained would have our mammy on instant alert.

"Yes, wee heart," I told her, as gently as I could, still trying to figure a way out of the bother she had landed us in. "A grand idea... Only there's a few problems with it, if Mammy finds out."

But Mammy wasn't *going* to find out...not if I could

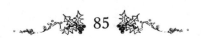

help it. All I had to do was hide Baby Jesus in the shoe box under my bed. I'd make sure I was first into school next morning, slip him back into the crib, and the Rocket wouldn't know Baby Jesus had been over-nighting, and Mammy wouldn't know, and my skin would be saved. As usual, I reckoned without our Rosaleen's funny mind.

"I *promised* Baby Jesus I'd take him to see his big mammy and daddy," she said, stubbornly, when I told her the plan.

"Well, you'll just have to break your promise," I said.

"It was *Baby Jesus* I promised," she said. "Baby Jesus is *special*. And Christmas is his birthday. So it was an extra-special-Christmas-birthday promise, not just an ordinary one."

The more I thought about it, the more she seemed to be right. The Baby Jesus *is* special. You can't go promising Jesus something and then not do it, can you? Especially at Christmas.

No time for messing about, or Mammy'd be down the

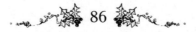

lane checking why we weren't home. If it was going to be done, it had to be now, this minute, before she noticed we hadn't turned up yet. I'd tell Mammy that I'd taken Rosaleen in to see the crib on our way past the church. It would only take five minutes to do that...and it would all be true, with only the Baby Jesus bit left out. Great...so long as no one spotted us doing it. That's why I needed Mickey.

So on the way to the church I hooked him off his football pitch. The two Gormans weren't pleased. They dripped off home with their ball, calling me bossy names. Mickey wasn't too happy either...but he was a lot less happy when he heard the full story.

"If anyone finds out what she's done, Christmas is cancelled for all of us!" Mickey moaned.

"Nobody is going to find out, Mickey," I told him.

He made a face. He's good at faces, Mickey.

"You've got to keep a look-out for us," I told him. "If someone comes in the church while we're doing

Rosaleen's Baby Jesus business, you head them off. It'll only take a minute. Then I'll get Rosaleen back to the house, no questions asked."

"How do I head this *someone* off?" Mickey asked.

"I don't know *how*," I told him, impatiently. "Depends *who* the *someone* is, and what happens. You'll have to figure out *how* when it happens, if it happens...but it probably won't happen anyway."

Wrong! It had to be cleaning afternoon, didn't it? There was old Boiler Morgan tottering round the church, held up by her mop and bucket, doing the aisles. It's lucky she didn't spot us standing at the door gaping at her.

Boiler is not fit to be a cleaner. She does it dead slowly. Mammy says her church work is the one thing the old lady loves doing, so Father Cleland lets her go on doing it, weak heart and all. The thing is, our house is next but one up the lane from the church: old Boiler knows our Mammy well, and she knows *us*. If she saw us, we'd be cooked. I needed old Boiler safely out of the way, while we did Rosaleen's Baby Jesus business.

"How will we get her out of the way?" Mickey asked, anxiously.

"I know," I said. "Remember last year, when you and the Gormans were snowballing round the back, and Boiler came out and stopped you? Do it again! Start shouting and chucking snowballs, and she'll come out to scold you. While she's doing that, Rosaleen will be in and out again, no bother, and nobody will be any the wiser!"

"Boiler said she'd tell our mammies if she caught us at it again," Mickey said, doubtfully.

"Pull your scarf up over your face, so she won't recognize you," I suggested. "And put your anorak hood up. She's as slow as a tortoise. She'll never get near you anyway."

"The Snow Phantom strikes again!" Mickey cried, getting into the spirit of the thing. He's a good brother in a crisis, our Mickey.

As disguises go, it wasn't all that successful. He still looked like our Mickey with a scarf round his nose to me,

but Boiler has big double-glazed specs so I hoped she wouldn't be able to recognize him.

Rosaleen and I waited in the church porch while the Snow Phantom crept round to the side door making a big deal out of the creeping bit. I whistled three times, which was the Snow-Phantom-Go signal we'd agreed. Mickey started banging snowballs against the church wall, and yelling in different voices, as though he was half a dozen Snow Phantoms in a fight. I took another look through the door, and sure enough Boiler was headed out to put a stop to the racket. Her legs move slowly, but in the end she made it through the door.

"Now!" I told Rosaleen.

We got up the aisle to the crib, on tippy toes. Rosaleen nearly tripped over Boiler's mop and yellow bucket in her excitement, but I managed to stop her in time.

"Do it!" I told her.

Rosaleen took the Baby Jesus out from under her

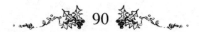

winter coat, and held him up in front of the crib.

"Look, Baby Jesus," she said. "There's your mammy and daddy."

That's when it all went wrong.

Mickey appeared in a flurry of snow and slush, running in through the side door. "Boiler's after me!" he yelled, and then he was down the aisle and away.

I didn't wait for Boiler to hobble slowly back in and catch us. I grabbed our Rosaleen and ran after Mickey. We followed him down the lane and out by the harbour, away from our house. The harbour is where I caught up with him, in our usual hidey-hole behind Gorman's lobster pots. I had to carry Rosaleen, because she has tiny legs and she couldn't keep up, and I ended up lugging her in my arms.

Mickey was full of himself. "I got old Boiler!" he told me. "Yes! Yes! Yes! I'll be a school legend for ever! Old Boiler's a snow woman now."

My breath nearly stopped. "You snowballed old Boiler

Morgan?" I said, thinking of her weak heart.

"Like you told me to," he said, cheerfully.

It was the church wall I'd told him to snowball, not the old woman. I opened my mouth to tell him so, then I shut it again, my brain going into overdrive. I went wobbly, inside. "You...we...we might have done something awful, Mickey." I said, slowly. "Suppose Boiler had a heart attack. Like the time before when Mammy had to get the ambulance to her?"

"I never meant to hurt her," Mickey said, anxiously. "It was only a laugh."

"Some laugh," I told him.

We ran back up the lane to the church, scared of what we would find when we got there. The church door was lying wide open, the way we'd left it.

"She's all right. She's gone home," Mickey said, hopefully.

"If she'd gone home she'd have shut the door," I told him. "She could be lying dead on the floor."

We went in. This time, the church was glittery-ghosty and really creepy, the way old churches can be. It felt very strange.

"I'm frightened," Rosaleen whispered, clinging on to me.

She wasn't the only one, but I didn't say so. "Mrs. Morgan? Mrs. Morgan?" I called, softly.

No sign of her...but her mop and bucket were still there, so she hadn't gone home. What had happened? Was she lying out there in the snow? Or was she...

"Where is she?" Mickey whispered. I don't know why we were all whispering...it just seemed a whispery place to be.

It was Rosaleen who found her. Old Boiler was slumped in one of the pews by the side altar, glasses off, gazing in front of her. She was breathing heavily, and looking flustered.

"Are you *dead*, Mrs. Morgan?" Rosaleen asked, with her eyes round as saucers.

Boiler turned her head slowly, which was a relief anyway, because it meant she wasn't dead...but she didn't look exactly pleased to see us, which wasn't surprising. Her overall was all snow down one side, and dripping wet as the snow melted.

I was so relieved that she wasn't dead that words came bursting out of me. "You-were-never-ever-ever-meant-to-be-snowballed-Mrs.-Morgan-and-we're-so-so-sorry-and-it-wasn't-supposed-to-happen-and-we-thought-you-might-be-dead-and-that's-why-we-came-back-and-now-you're-all-right-and-we're-everso-sorry-Mrs.-Morgan-and-we-won't-never-ever-do-anything-like-that-ever-ever-ever-again," I said.

Rosaleen started crying...and I'm certain-sure it was Rosaleen crying that saved us. At the sight of her little tear-stained face puckering up, Boiler roused herself, and came over all concerned. Old ladies always seem to do that with our Rosaleen. They don't know her like I do.

"There, there. Don't cry, wee pet," Boiler told her, gently.

"I promised our Baby Jesus from school I'd take him

to see the one in the church and we did...and..." Rosaleen sobbed, as the old lady hugged her.

What did she have to mention the school's Baby Jesus for? Just when it looked as if her tears would get us out of the snowballing trouble, Rosaleen *had* to dump us back in it again. There was nothing I could do but explain the whole thing.

"Show Mrs. Morgan your Baby Jesus," I told Rosaleen, reluctantly, when I'd finished.

Rosaleen felt inside her winter coat, and then her face crumpled up, and she was off again... This time the tears really flowed.

"I've lost wee Baby Jesus!" she sobbed.

"You haven't!" I said, my heart going down to my boots.

"Yes, I have," she said. "I've lost Baby Jesus."

It was Old Boiler who rose to the occasion this time. "We'll have to look for him then, won't we dear?" she said, and the old lady gave Rosaleen another hug and then took

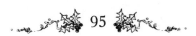

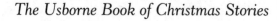

her by the hand and went Baby-Jesus-Hunting, up and down the aisle and round the pews.

We hunted with her, and then Rosaleen and Mickey and I searched down the lane to the harbour and back, checking the hedges and in our hidey-hole behind Gorman's lobster pots, just in case, while Boiler hobbled slowly round inside the church, having a second look.

When we got back to the church, Boiler was waiting for us. I should have realized she was up to something from the odd look on her face, but I didn't...not then. I was too busy wondering what *exactly* schools do to kids who take their Baby Jesus home for the night and then manage to lose him.

"Our Baby Jesus is lost and gone for ever!" Rosaleen wailed, over-egging the drama, as usual.

"If you close your eyes and wish very hard, then maybe you'll find him. Make it a special Christmas wish," Boiler suggested.

I looked at Mickey, and he shrugged.

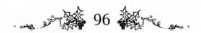

Rosaleen closed her eyes, and wished very hard, using her best Christmas wish, as instructed.

"You two big O'Hares as well," Boiler told us, with a gleam in her eye that showed through the double-glazed specs.

We didn't think it would work, but we closed our eyes anyway. I suppose I was half hoping that when we opened them, the school Baby Jesus would be there in front of us...but that is Christmas miracle stuff like in some old movie, and it didn't happen.

"No Baby Jesus!" Rosaleen said.

"Maybe you're just not looking in the right place," Boiler suggested.

"We've looked *everywhere* there is," Rosaleen said.

"Where would you expect to find a baby, pet?" Boiler asked gently...and suddenly I guessed what the old lady was up to.

"In his cot?" Rosaleen said.

"What cot?" said Mickey.

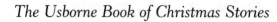

The Usborne Book of Christmas Stories

But Rosaleen was already headed for the church crib.
And that's where she found the wee Baby Jesus...lying in
the manger – which is a kind of cot, I suppose. It was all
the cot the real Baby Jesus had, anyway.

"Wee Baby Jesus is here!" Rosaleen shouted.

"I *looked* all round the crib and our Baby Jesus wasn't
there," I told old Boiler, accusingly. "Someone must have
put him there!"

"*Someone?*" she said, and she winked at me. "You'd
better get him back where he belongs, before his mammy
and daddy notice that he's gone missing," Boiler told
Rosaleen.

That was it. The wee Baby Jesus slept over in a shoe box
under Rosaleen's bed. Next morning we got ourselves into
school very early and put the Baby Jesus back in the crib
before anyone knew he'd been on his Christmas holidays.

"Don't you ever go telling Mammy or Miss O'Neill
or any of the grown-ups, what happened," I told our
Rosaleen.

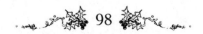

She agreed, but she still looked a bit glum.

"What's wrong now?" I asked, impatiently.

"I used up my best Christmas wish on Baby Jesus," Rosaleen said. "Does that mean my other ones won't come true?"

"I suppose they might, if you wish very hard," I told her.

And on Christmas Day, they did.

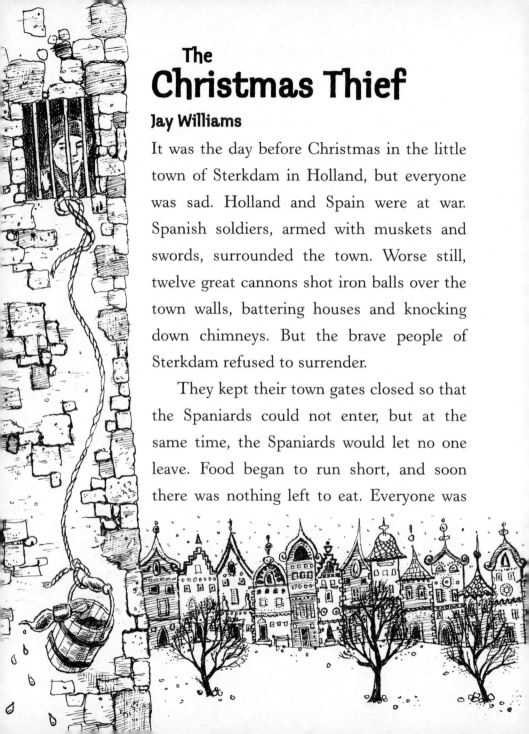

The
Christmas Thief

Jay Williams

It was the day before Christmas in the little town of Sterkdam in Holland, but everyone was sad. Holland and Spain were at war. Spanish soldiers, armed with muskets and swords, surrounded the town. Worse still, twelve great cannons shot iron balls over the town walls, battering houses and knocking down chimneys. But the brave people of Sterkdam refused to surrender.

They kept their town gates closed so that the Spaniards could not enter, but at the same time, the Spaniards would let no one leave. Food began to run short, and soon there was nothing left to eat. Everyone was hungry, from the mayor in his fine house to the only prisoner in the town jail.

This prisoner's name was Tyl Uilenspiegel, and he was a famous thief. It was said that he could steal the eggs from under a sitting hen, or the spectacles off your nose. In Sterkdam there was little to steal, and Tyl had let the officers arrest him and put him in prison so that he would have food and shelter for the winter. Now, however, they could not give him so much as a crust of bread.

He stood at the barred window, looked at the clear blue sky, and sighed. A boy walked by in the street below, hugging his stomach and weeping. Tyl heard him and looked down. "What's the matter with you?" he asked.

"I'm hungry," said the boy, "and tomorrow is Christmas. There will be no presents and no Christmas dinner. Not even Saint Nicholas could get into this town with the Spaniards all around it."

Tyl stared at the boy and thought about all the hungry children of Sterkdam. "Maybe I can do something about it," he said. "Get me a pail of blue paint and a brush, and come back here as quickly as you can."

Away sped the boy. Soon he returned with the paint and brush. Around his waist Tyl always carried a long, thin cord. He uncoiled it now and lowered it through the bars.

"Put the brush in the pail and tie the handle of the pail to the cord," he said.

When the boy had done so, Tyl pulled up the pail. He painted the bars of his window blue; then he stood in a corner behind the cell door and shouted, loudly, "Goodbye! I'm going!"

The guard heard him and came running. He unlocked the door and opened it. When he looked in he saw a window without bars – for the blue bars did not show against the blue sky. "The prisoner has escaped!" he cried, and rushed off for help, leaving the cell door open. Tyl strolled quietly out of the prison and into the street, taking with him a sheet from his bed.

There were people guarding the walls of the town, and

there were more people guarding the great main gate. And there was one man with a musket guarding the little iron door that opened onto the river.

Tyl walked up to him and said, "What are you doing?"

The guard straightened. "My orders are not to let anyone in through the gate," he replied.

"Very good," said Tyl. "Then open it, for I am already in, and I am going out."

The man unbolted the gate. "The Spaniards will kill you," he warned.

"They will if they see me," said Tyl, "but I won't let them see me."

He put the bed sheet over his head. Against the white snow he was invisible. He walked to the frozen river and crossed it.

In the Spanish camp the soldiers were preparing their Christmas Eve feast, roasting meat and cooking good stews in big iron pots over blazing bonfires. Tyl crept up to the back of the nearest tent, and with a tiny knife slit the canvas. He peeped in; there was no one inside. He stepped through the slit. When he came out of the front of the tent, he was wearing a Spanish helmet and breastplate and carrying a big cloak over one arm.

He walked boldly to one of the fires and helped himself to a piece of roast meat. One of the soldiers stopped him and said, "Where are you going with that?"

"It is for the general," answered Tyl in his best Spanish. He put the meat into the cloak. He went to another fire and took a roast chicken. "For the general," he said.

When he could carry no more, he found a quiet corner and hid the food. Then off he went again with the empty cloak – as lightly as a feather, as quietly as a puff of smoke – taking candies and cakes, strings of sausages, loaves of bread, round hard cheeses, roast geese, legs of lamb, and slices of beef.

From the general's tent, Tyl took an enormous Christmas pudding. As he was leaving with the pudding wrapped in his cloak, a soldier said, "Wait.

What have you there?"

"A present from the general to the captain," said Tyl, and went on his way.

As darkness fell, the Spaniards deserted their posts to eat dinner. Tyl went up to the first cannon. It was loaded and ready, pointing at the town wall. He took out the cannonball and in its place crammed a bundle of food. He did the same to the next cannon, and the next, until all twelve were filled with food instead of cannonballs. Then he went looking for the captain of artillery.

"Sir," said Tyl, saluting. "I bring a message from the general. You are to fire all your cannons at the city tonight to show the people of Sterkdam they can have no rest."

"But how can we aim in the darkness?" asked the captain of artillery.

"I will sneak into the town and light a torch in the church tower," said Tyl. "You can aim at the light, and you must fire all the cannons together, just once."

"You are a brave man," said the captain.

"I know," said Tyl modestly. "Be ready for my signal."
He took off the helmet and armour. Then, like the shadow
of an owl, he slipped back across the river.

Near the town walls stood a tall windmill, its sails
turning slowly in the night breeze. Tyl jumped up and
caught the lowest sail. Up he went, higher and higher,
until he was level with the top of the wall. Then he leaped
with all his might and fell sprawling on the hard stone. No
one saw him. The town was quiet. The hungry people had
gone to bed early.

Tyl climbed down and made his way to the town
square. There he pounded on people's doors, shouting,
"Wake up! Wake up! Come out! Come out!"

Windows flew open. People looked and shouted,
"What is it? What's happening?" They came into the
street with swords and torches and lanterns, thinking the
Spanish army was attacking.

Tyl snatched a torch from someone and ran up the
steps of the church. He stood before the door where

everyone could see him. "Listen!" he cried. "Saint Nicholas is coming."

The mayor was there in his nightcap. "It's the thief, Tyl Uilenspiegel," he exclaimed. "Seize him! Arrest him!"

"Wait—" Tyl began.

But several men were already advancing on him, swords ready. Tyl turned, ran into the church, slammed the door in their faces, and bolted it.

Up the tower stairs he raced, until he came to the top where the great bells hung. He leaned out, waving his torch. The townspeople stared up at him with their mouths open.

"Shoot him," commanded the mayor. "He is signalling to the enemy."

Muskets were raised; men took aim. But before they could fire a shot – *boom!* came the crash of the Spanish cannons. And out of the sky fell roast geese, roast chickens, roast beef, and loaves of bread. Nuts and candies pattered down like hail; cheeses bounced off the rooftops. A leg of lamb fell into a woman's arms. A string of sausages wrapped itself around a man's neck. The general's plum pudding hit the mayor on the head, knocking him flat.

"Merry Christmas!" yelled Tyl, leaning from the tower.

Everyone cheered and hurried to pick up the good things. Then a bonfire was lit in the square, and the people of Sterkdam feasted until dawn.

As the bells rang out on Christmas morning, an army of Hollanders came marching across the plains towards the town. There were too many of them for the Spaniards, who ran away without a fight – leaving their tents, their cooking pots, and even their cannons behind. The gates of the town were opened at last, and the people welcomed their friends with joy.

That night, in a solemn ceremony, the mayor hung a golden chain around Tyl's neck. On it was a golden medal inscribed with these words:

> *To the thief Tyl Uilenspiegel who stole*
> *Christmas for the people of Sterkdam.*

The Worst Christmas Ever

Malorie Blackman

I'm only writing this because Mr. Cooling, my teacher, says I have to. I don't particularly want to write about my Christmas. It was the worst Christmas ever. I know everyone in my class thinks I'm lucky because I always get everything I want – but that all changed this Christmas. I really don't want to talk about this. It still upsets me to think about it – and I think about it a lot. But as I don't seem to have much choice – here goes.

Two or three weeks before Christmas, Mum and Dad sat me down in my own special armchair. They sat opposite me on the sofa. I smiled at them. I knew what was going to come next, or at least, I thought I did.

"You're going to ask me what I want for Christmas, aren't you?" I said, excited. "I've already made my Christmas list. I want the new computer game, the one called—"

"Kathini, we're not here to talk about Christmas presents," Dad interrupted.

That was when I noticed their faces. Mum and Dad looked so sad and sombre.

"What's the matter?" I asked.

"It's very difficult, darling," Mum began. "It's about the company we own..."

"Yes," I said impatiently.

"Well, our company hasn't been doing too well recently and now we're going to have to close it down completely."

"For how long?" I asked.

"For good," Dad replied.

"But...but then what will I get for Christmas?" I asked.

Mum and Dad looked at each other.

"I'm sure we'll be able to manage something—" Dad began, but Mum interrupted him.

"We have to face facts, dear," she said to Dad. Then she turned to me. "Kathini, we're not sure we'll even be able to afford Christmas this year. We're going to have to move out of our house and we'll all have to tighten our belts."

"What does that mean?" I asked.

"We're going to have to make do. With everything we've got, we're going to have to use it up and wear it out," said Mum.

I looked at both of them. Dad bent his head. Mum sat with a stony expression on her face.

"You're joking – right?" I knew she wasn't but I had to ask anyway.

"We haven't got any money," Mum said, her voice as hard as stone. "We're going to have one gigantic sale and sell off all the toys and games we have left in our factory. If we sell enough we might just clear our debts but there'll be no money left over for luxuries – and Christmas is a luxury."

I jumped to my feet. "How could you? HOW COULD YOU?" I screamed at Mum and Dad. "I'm not going to have a proper Christmas and it's all your fault."

And I raced from the room, tears streaming down my face. After that, I barely spoke to Mum and Dad. We had all kinds of strangers tramping through our house, looking in my bedroom and all over. The fifth couple who came to look at our house said that they would buy it. I hated them too. How could they move into our house? Someone else would have *my* room. I cried and cried myself to sleep each night, but it didn't make any difference. Mum and Dad said they had to sell the house and that was that.

Mum and Dad decided to hold their toy sale on

Christmas Eve, which was a Friday. They spent the days before Christmas Eve writing up lots of posters to advertise their sale. They put the ads all over the town where we lived.

In spite of all my wishing and hoping, Christmas Eve arrived far too soon. Mum and Dad were getting ready for their big toy sell-off.

"Come on, Kathini. Put on your coat and gloves," said Dad.

"No, I won't." I shook my head and crossed my arms. "I'm going to stay here."

"You can't stay here by yourself," Mum said firmly.

"Yes, I can," I argued.

"Kathini, you're going to come with us even if I have to carry you," said Mum. "This is hard enough on your dad and me as it is, without you making it ten times harder."

My eyes started stinging when Mum said that, so to cover it up I scowled even harder. It was no use – Mum and Dad insisted that I had to help them sell all the toys and games they had left in their factory.

"I'm surprised you haven't asked me to sell all my toys as well," I sniffed.

"It might just come to that," Dad muttered.

I don't think I was meant to hear that bit, but I did.

Once we reached the warehouse, it took an hour for Mum and Dad to set everything up. All the toys Mum and Dad owned were set up on huge tables at the front of the building. Other grown-ups who worked at the factory were also there to help out, including Mr. Johnson who's a good friend of my parents.

"What's the matter, Kathini? Why the long face?" he asked.

"It's not fair. I hope no one buys a thing," I sulked.

"Well, for your mum and dad's sake, I hope for once you *don't* get what you want," Mr. Johnson replied, coldly.

Ignoring him, I sat on a chair behind one of the tables and watched as the gates were opened to the public. The tables were covered with a lot of toys I already had and some I didn't. Each toy had a price tag attached to it and I could see at once that most of the toys were less than half price.

It wasn't fair. It wasn't *right*. Where would all my toys come from in the future if Mum and Dad had to sell everything?

But half an hour later, I began to smile. We'd only had a few people on to the forecourt of the factory and only a couple of them had bought anything.

Let's hope no one else will turn up, I thought to myself.

And that's when I saw him – a boy, about my age. He wore tatty, patched trousers, a jumper with holes in it and a dirty anorak that wasn't zipped up. He wandered in my direction, his eyes huge as he took in everything on the table.

"This is amazing," he said when he'd reached me.

"Huh!" I answered.

"I wish I could afford just one thing here," he sighed.

"Not for me, but for my brother."

"If you can't afford anything you should go away," I told him.

"I can at least look," he told me. "Looking is free."

I glowered at the boy, wishing he would leave.

"So what's your name?" the boy asked.

"Kathini." I didn't ask him what his name was. I thought he might get the hint from that – but he didn't.

"I'm Ileo," he smiled.

"That's a strange name. I've never heard that before," I couldn't help admitting.

"My dad said he chose it because it means 'I Love Everyone'," Ileo said proudly. "I like your name too. It's pretty. It suits you. Kathini..."

My face went all warm when he said that.

"Thanks," I smiled.

I don't know why but for the first time I noticed his clenched hands. He'd made fists against the icy weather in an effort to keep his fingers warm. The skin around his knuckles was pinched and wrinkled with the cold. I had on thick sheepskin mittens and I could still feel the Christmas chill. At that moment all I could think about was how uncomfortable his hands must be. My smile faded at the thought.

"What's the matter?" Ileo asked. He leaned forward, anxious to hear my reply. "You don't look very happy."

I didn't want to embarrass him by mentioning his hands so with a sigh, I pointed to the table in front of me.

"Mum and Dad – they have to sell all this stuff."

"Where did they get it all from?"

"They made it in their factory over there," I replied. "But now they're having to sell the factory and these toys and our house 'cause they don't have any money."

"I'm sorry."

And Ileo really did look sorry too.

"So much for Christmas," I sniffed, fighting back the tears.

"What d'you mean?"

"We won't have any money to do *anything*," I said angrily. I would've thought it was obvious what I meant.

"What does Christmas mean to you then?" Ileo asked, surprised.

"Lots of presents, lots of food, staying up late, good things like that."

"No wonder you're so miserable," Ileo smiled. "You've got it all wrong."

"What d'you mean?"

"Christmas isn't about what you get. Christmas is about what you *give* – and I don't just mean things either."

"You can't give anything except things," I said, confused.

"Not true. You can give love, friendship, happiness. Things like that. Too many people think that all they need to make them happy is money and the things it can buy."

"Money does make people happy. If Mum and Dad had money we'd be happy now," I said.

"You think so?" Ileo asked me. "I bet your mum and

dad worked so hard here that you didn't see them as often as you would've liked."

"They bought me lots of presents to make up for it."

"What would you rather have? Presents or your parents?"

I blinked with surprise. I'd never thought of it that way before.

"My dad says that too many people nowadays have forgotten how Christmas started and what it's really about," said Ileo.

"You mean that it's the day Jesus Christ was born?" I said doubtfully.

"But it's more than that. Imagine millions and millions of people all over the world celebrating one person's birthday – isn't that amazing!" said Ileo. "My dad says birthdays should be celebrated and enjoyed – not sweated over and cursed because they're so much expense and hard work. My dad says that was never what Christmas was meant to be about."

"I guess..." I hadn't really thought about that either.

"Anyway, I didn't mean to bend your ear." Ileo shrugged. "I'd better get home before everyone wonders where I've got to."

Ileo turned to leave. I looked around. Mum and Dad were nowhere in sight and the nearest grown-up was at least four tables away.

"Ileo, hang on. Would...would you like one of these toys?" I indicated the toys on the long table before me.

"Can't afford them," Ileo said cheerfully.

"You can take one if you'd like. You don't have to pay for it. Mum and Dad won't mind," I said.

"Are you sure?" Ileo raised his eyebrows.

I nodded. "Go ahead. Happy Christmas!"

Ileo picked up a model-making kit and hugged it to his chest.

"Great! Thanks! It's very kind of you. My brother will love it."

I started to grin at the look on Ileo's face. I couldn't

help it. He was so happy. And the funny thing is – it seemed to rub off on me.

"Take something for yourself as well," I smiled.

"Are you sure?"

"Yeah! Go on."

"Are you sure you're sure?" Ileo asked, astounded.

"Go ahead. I want you to."

Ileo picked up another model-making kit, clutching it as if he'd never let it go.

I gasped with shock. "What's the matter with your hands?"

Ileo had an angry-looking scar on the back of each hand. I hadn't noticed them before but now I wondered how I could've missed them.

"The scars go all the way through – see!" Ileo raised one hand to show me his palm. The scar did indeed go all the way through to his palm.

"How did you do that? Does it hurt?" I asked, concerned.

"All the time," Ileo shrugged. "But I don't mind. I'd

better get going. Just wait till my brother sees this! Not to mention my dad."

"Ileo, wait! Hang on a—" But it was too late. Off he raced. As I watched him go, I felt really strange. Yes, I was sad about the scars on his hands but he'd left me feeling... not just happy, but *glad* inside. It's hard to describe. It was like a light switching on inside me. That's the only way I can think of it.

"Are you okay, Kathini?" Dad appeared from nowhere to stand beside me.

I smiled at him.

"Well, I'm glad to see you've cheered up a bit," Dad smiled. "I'm sorry about this. It's not going to be much of a Christmas for you I'm afraid."

"How're we doing?" I asked.

"Not very well," Dad sighed. "I think we're still going to have most of this stuff at the end of the day."

"And then what will happen to it?" I asked.

"The new owners of the factory will probably dump

the lot. They're going to use the factory for something else so they don't want toys cluttering up the place," Dad explained.

"And if you sell all this stuff, will it get you and Mum out of trouble?" I asked.

"Not really. But we'll be able to have a decent Christmas. We'll be able to buy you lots of presents and we'll have lots of food. It'll be our best Christmas ever before we have to move house."

I took a look around. "But no one's here to buy any of it."

"I know." Dad's shoulders slumped as he too looked around.

"Dad, I know a way to get rid of it," I told him.

"How?"

"We could give it away," I said.

Dad stared at me. "Pardon?"

"Can we give it away, Dad?" I rushed on as Dad opened his mouth to argue. "No one's buying it anyway and lots of people would be glad of your toys. You make brilliant toys, Dad. So if we can't sell them, we could give them to people who really want them. Then they wouldn't end up on a rubbish dump somewhere."

"I...I don't know..."

Dad looked doubtful but I could see that he was having a serious think about it.

"Let me go and ask your mum," Dad said at last. Five minutes later, Mum, Dad and all the other grown-ups were crowding around my table.

"I can't believe it!"

"Kathini, this was *your* idea?"

My face started to burn. For the first time, I actually listened to what they were saying. Before I heard what they were saying about me, but I didn't really listen – and because I didn't listen, I didn't take any notice. But now it was obvious what most of them thought of me. They thought I was selfish and spoilt and only thought about myself. And the worse thing was, they were absolutely right.

Mum smiled at me. "Would you really like us to give away these toys?" she asked.

I nodded, shyly.

"Well, I think that's a wonderful idea," said Dad.

"So do I," Mr. Johnson agreed. He stared at me as if he couldn't quite believe that it had been my idea.

Mum said very softly, "Kathini, I'm proud of you."

And that's how we got our picture in the local newspaper.

We loaded up all the toys into large bin liners and set off to the shopping precinct. Whilst the grown-ups were wondering what to do next, I stepped forward and shouted at the top of my lungs, "Merry Christmas! Come and get some free toys. Merry Christmas!"

At first, not many people stopped. They must've thought it was a trick or something. But then one woman with her two children stopped, then a man with his son and soon we were surrounded and we couldn't give them away fast enough. But then two policemen arrived.

"Who's in charge here?" asked one of them.

Dad moved forwards.

"One of the toy shops in the precinct called us. You can't sell goods here without a licence," the policeman told him.

"I'm not selling these toys. I'm giving them away," Dad explained.

The policeman frowned at him. "If they're not safe, you can't give them away either."

"They're perfectly safe," said Dad. "They conform to all the rules and regulations regarding safe toys. We made them in our factory but as the factory is closing down for good in the New Year, we thought we'd give the toys away."

"That's very Christmassy of you!" said the other policeman.

Dad grinned at him. "We think so! It was all my daughter's idea."

And after that the two policemen helped us to give

out the presents. Someone else must have called the local newspaper because within fifteen minutes we were all having our photographs taken. I've never had such a wonderful time. It was...magic! You should've seen the looks on people's faces when they got their toys. So many people came up to Mum and Dad and thanked them.

"I was wondering how I'd find the money to buy my son something for Christmas and now, thanks to you..."

"How can I ever thank you?" said another. "I just didn't have the money to buy toys this Christmas."

And as I watched the smiling faces all around us, it was like the light in me was burning brighter and brighter. It was such fun. Ileo was right.

When we got home that night, Mum and Dad were in a better mood than they'd been for a long time.

"Well, we didn't make a bean but I'm kind of glad," said Dad as he flopped down on to the sofa.

"It was good, wasn't it," Mum agreed. "At least we went out with a bang!"

Dad ordered a pizza and after we'd all eaten, I went to bed – for once without protesting about it. I had a lot to think about.

Christmas Day was sunny and bright. I looked out of my bedroom window over our back garden and it was as if I was seeing it for the first time. It was so beautiful. The bare trees waved gently in the wind. It was as if they were wishing me a good morning. I'd never noticed them before and now it was too late. I watched the trees for a long, long while. Then I had my shower and went down for breakfast.

"Happy Christmas, Kathini." Mum and Dad grinned at me as soon as I entered the living room.

"Happy Christmas!" I replied. And I gave them both a kiss on the cheek.

"Open your present then," said Mum.

"I didn't think you'd bought me anything," I said, surprised.

"It's only small," Dad apologized.

"That doesn't matter," I smiled.

I opened my present. Usually for Christmas I got at least six or seven presents, but now I didn't mind that I'd only got one. And what a present it was! It was a dark purple jumper, covered with gold and silver embroidered stars. It was amazing, I put it on at once.

"And I've got something for both of you," I said slowly.

"What's that?"

"I want to say I'm sorry. I'm sorry that you've had to close down your factory and I'm sorry that I only thought about myself when you told me. I didn't mean to be such a brat." I felt like crying when I remembered all the horrible things I'd said and done. Looking back I couldn't believe it was the same person.

"What's brought all this about?" Mum asked me.

"Something Ileo said to me," I admitted.

"Who's Ileo?" Dad asked.

"The boy I was talking to yesterday at the factory, before we went to the precinct," I replied.

Dad frowned. "I didn't see you talking with any boy —
and I was keeping an eye on you."

"You must have seen him. He was wearing old, worn-
out clothes and his hair needed combing," I said.

"Kathini, your mum and I were keeping an eye on you
all the time we were on the factory forecourt. We never
saw you talk to anyone, except Mr. Johnson," said Dad.

"You must've missed him then," I frowned. "It's a
shame, because Ileo was so nice. I gave him a toy for
himself and his brother."

"Good for you. And thank you, Ileo — whoever and
wherever you may be," Mum smiled.

Mum, Dad and I had a wonderful Christmas. We
played board games and stuffed our faces and cuddled up
on the sofa to watch some films on the TV. I was so happy
I couldn't stop smiling. None of us could. And that's
when I knew that no matter what happened, as long as we
were together, we'd be all right.

Well, since then, we've had our picture in the paper

and then our story and picture appeared in a national newspaper and caused quite a stir. We were very popular with everyone but the owners of the toy shops in the precinct. And d'you know what happened in the New Year? Because of the picture in the paper, this man called Mr. Gardner came to see my mum and dad. He said he'd like to go into partnership with them because they'd generated so much publicity that *everyone* wants our toys. Mum and Dad's factory was saved and we managed to keep our house.

Everything turned out okay in the end. So why do I call it my worst Christmas ever? Because it still makes me cringe to think about how I behaved before Christmas. It still makes my face burn to remember how much of a...a brat I was!

But I have changed. The only thing I wish now is that I could see Ileo again. I find I'm thinking about him a lot – every day. He said that Ileo stood for "I Love Everyone". I think that's wonderful. The strange thing is, I find myself talking to him in my head and I sometimes feel he actually talks back to me. It's as if we've always been friends and always will be. Isn't that strange? And isn't it sad that it took all the things that happened at Christmas for me to know him and to listen to him. But as I'm sure Ileo would say – better late than never. And do you know what the best thing about talking to Ileo in my head is? I'll tell you. When I talk to him I feel happy and every day is Christmas.

Little Plum Duff

Jean Chapman

Mr. Duffy drove a delivery truck for one of the city stores. Christmas was a busy time for him. So many parcels had to be delivered to people's houses. Big ones, fat ones, heavy ones, lumpy ones!

While he was out one morning, fine misty rain began to fall. Swish-swish went his windscreen wipers as he drove along. "Drat it!" grumbled Mr. Duffy as the rain became heavier. "I've forgotten my raincoat."

So, when he came to the next house, he made a fast dash for its door with a parcel under his arm. The truck's cabin door swung open.

A little stray cat looked into the cabin. It was dry inside. In jumped the cat. He shook his wet paws, he shook the raindrops from his fur and then settled down under the dashboard. *"Prrrr,"* said the cat.

Mr. Duffy raced back to his truck, pulled the door shut and drove on to make his next delivery. He didn't see the cat. In fact, he was too busy to notice the cat all through the morning. The cat did not make a sound.

By lunchtime Mr. Duffy was back in the city. He stopped for some traffic lights, waiting in a line of cars and other trucks.

"Meouw!" said the cat.

Mr. Duffy looked to the footpath, expecting to see a cat. But there were only people walking along. No cat! People were crossing the street, too. No cat was with them. He looked at the car waiting beside him. Only a man was in it. No cat!

"Funny, I thought I heard a cat," said Mr. Duffy.

The traffic lights turned green then. *Brrrummm!* Mr. Duffy was on his way again.

"Meouw!" said the cat in a thin high voice, too high and thin to be heard over the engine's sound. "Meww!" said the cat and jumped up on the seat beside Mr. Duffy. It rubbed its head against his arm.

"Lumme!" exploded Mr. Duffy. "The cat's in my truck!"

"Mewwwwww!" answered the cat.

It was no use Mr. Duffy saying, "Get, Cat! Scat!" Not in town traffic. He didn't know where it had come from. He didn't know what to do with it. And it was such a skinny little cat. He took it back to the store where he ate his lunch. The cat watched Mr. Duffy bite into a sandwich. "Meouw!" it pleaded.

Mr. Duffy took another bite.

"Meouwww!" cried the cat, staring at the sandwich.

"Cats don't eat cheese," said Mr. Duffy, tossing it some cheese from his bread. But that cat did eat cheese, all the cheese in Mr. Duffy's lunch. And Mr. Duffy ate bread-and-butter.

Mr. Duffy drank strong black tea. The cat drank the milk he usually poured into it. Then it curled up on some wrapping paper and went to sleep.

All the week the cat stayed in the storeroom. Mr. Duffy brought it meat and milk from home each day, right up to Christmas Eve. On Christmas Eve, just before he left the store, Mr. Duffy set out a pile of meat and a big bowl of milk, enough food to last the cat for at least three days, three holidays.

"That will keep you going until I come back after the Christmas break," he told the skinny little cat. Then Mr. Duffy set off for the bus stop. "Would that milk stay fresh?" he asked himself. No, it would not, not for three days! And the meat wouldn't either. Maybe the skinny little cat would eat all the meat at once and then be hungry before the next evening. "How can I eat my Christmas dinner if that cat is hungry?" thought Mr. Duffy. He turned about and went back to the store.

He picked up the skinny little cat, looking about for something to carry it in. There were plenty of paper bags and large sheets of paper. Nothing else! He put the cat into a big roomy bag, and with its head poking out from the top they went to the bus stop.

"Mewwww!" howled the skinny little cat.

"Now, look here, Mate, you can't take that cat on the bus," said the conductor. "No cats allowed on this bus."

"But it's Christmas, can't..." mumbled Mr. Duffy.

"No cats on the bus!" said the driver this time. "Sorry, Mate!"

"No cats in this taxi," said a taxi driver when Mr. Duffy hailed his cab.

So Mr. Duffy, with the skinny cat in a paper bag, walked home.

It was late when he went through his door. His dinner

was spoiled. His wife didn't scold. She was glad to see him home and gave him a kiss. Mr. Duffy's little girl kissed him too, and his little boy hugged and hugged him.

"I couldn't leave this skinny little chap in the store over Christmas," Mr. Duffy told his wife sheepishly.

"We'll keep him," she said. "He's no one's cat."

"He's our Christmas cat!" corrected the children.

Within weeks the skinny little Christmas cat had grown into a round, fat, contented Christmas cat with glossy dark fur and bright eyes. Mr. Duffy called him his little Plum Duff, the old name for a Christmas pudding. And Plum Duff is still with the family to this very day.

The Boy who was afraid of Father Christmas

Julia Jarman

Timothy Wilson wasn't a timid boy. He wasn't afraid of the dark or the dentist. He wasn't afraid of the big dipper at the funfair nor the roller coaster. He went on them both twice, and on the ghost train, which was very creepy. Lucy Wilson, Timothy's older sister, wouldn't go on the ghost train. She said it was S-C-A-R-Y.

At school, Timothy wasn't afraid of reading in front of everyone in assembly, nor jumping into the pool in swimming lessons. He wasn't afraid of the enormous spider in the boys' toilets. He wasn't a wimp. There was only one thing that scared him – strangers. And that was sensible, he thought, because everyone warned him about strangers.

His mum and dad were always telling him to be careful, when his dad was home, that is. Mr. Wilson worked on an oilrig in the middle of the North Sea so he was only home sometimes. Timothy missed him a lot. He wrote to his dad every week, and always sent him a packet of his favourite extra-strong peppermint sweets. His dad said they helped to keep out the cold when the north winds blew.

Teachers warned about strangers, and so did PC Watson, who showed the whole school a film called "Stranger Danger". The policeman said you mustn't talk to strangers and you mustn't take sweets or anything from them and you must never *never* go off with them. Timothy didn't want to go off with them. His grandma said that if a stranger offered Timothy or Lucy a sweet – or anything – they should shout very loudly the worst word they could think of, and run.

PC Watson said real burglars didn't wear striped shirts and masks like Burglar Bill, and real strangers didn't always look strange. Strangers often looked liked ordinary people, and they usually pretended to be nice. Some strangers did wear a disguise though, and some strangers weren't strangers. They were people you knew very well who suddenly acted *strangely*. It was complicated, so you had to be careful. That's why Timothy didn't want to write to Father Christmas. He didn't *know* Father Christmas. He didn't want him coming into his bedroom in the middle of the night.

Lucy wrote her letter to Father Christmas at school. She brought it home to post it up the chimney. Grandma said she would help Timothy write his letter, but Timothy

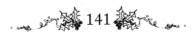

said, "No thank you, Grandma, I don't want to."

Lucy said, "If you don't write to Father Christmas he won't bring you any presents."

That was worrying, but not as worrying as having a stranger in your room. Why didn't anyone else worry?

Timothy wasn't afraid of the Father Christmas in Braggins store. Simon Barnes said that wasn't the real Father Christmas, and Timothy thought Simon was right because there was a Father Christmas in his grotto at Braggins and another one in his grotto at T. J. Howes. Suzy Wilkins went to see another Father Christmas in a big toy shop in London. Besides, when you went to see Father Christmas in his grotto your mum could come in with you. Timothy went in by himself because he saw other children coming out looking happy – and he got a model aeroplane kit. It was definitely only the real Father Christmas who scared him.

As Christmas got nearer he felt even worse, especially at night, because he couldn't help thinking about

Christmas Eve. It was hard to get to sleep. One morning he yawned at breakfast and his mum said, "Oh dear, Timothy, are you too excited to sleep?"

Lucy said, "He's not excited. He's S-C-A-R-E-D."

Timothy shouted, "I'm not!" Because if Lucy told everyone at school he'd be teased. Nobody else at all seemed scared, not even Linda Lumsden who said, "D-d-don't," if you even *mentioned* worms.

Lucy said, "I meant you're scared of not getting any presents, silly, because you didn't write a letter."

And Grandma said, "Well, Timothy doesn't need to worry about presents. I wrote and told Father Christmas what he wanted. He *will* come."

Christmas was coming – fast, too fast. One day Lucy opened ten doors of her advent calendar and ate all the chocolates behind them – to make Christmas come faster, she said! At school the teachers talked about Christmas all the time. Everyone in Timothy's class had to make Christmas cards and Christmas candle-holders

and Christmas snowmen full of sweets. The whole school had to practise singing Christmas carols every day – for the Christmas concert and the Christmas play. On the night of the Christmas play Mum came home from work with a Christmas tree.

"Only one week to go," she said, as she got the Christmas decorations out of the attic.

Next day, Timothy and Lucy broke up from school. When they got home Mum asked them to decorate the tree, while she made the Christmas puddings – though Gran said she'd left it far too late. Everyone had to have a wishing stir of the pudding mixture. Timothy made two wishes. One: that Father Christmas would leave the presents downstairs. Two: that his dad would come home for Christmas.

Time seemed to pass even faster now that the Christmas holiday was here. There was so much to do. Timothy and Lucy had to help decorate the house and deliver Christmas cards to the neighbours and wrap the

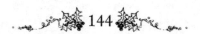

presents they had made for the family. On the day before Christmas Eve, Timothy found Lucy in her room, giggling. She was wrapping up the present she had made for him. It was cube-shaped. She wouldn't tell him what it was. She giggled even more when she put it under the tree, where the family put their presents for each other. Timothy went upstairs to his bedroom and closed the door. He had something important to do. He'd planned it carefully. Now he had to get on – with his Father Christmas Early Warning Device.

It was even more important now. He'd had some bad news. It looked as if Dad would not be home for Christmas. There were storms in the North Sea and helicopters couldn't leave the rig. It looked as if wishes didn't come true.

It took ages to get all the pieces and fix them together. The bell was the important bit. It was an old school bell which had belonged to Grandma long ago when she was a teacher. It was very loud. Children could hear it from the

end of the road, she said. Timothy attached it to a length of elastic. Then he hid it under the bed, ready for when he needed it.

On Christmas Eve, Lucy hurried to bed to hang up her stocking. Timothy stayed up as late as he could. He put his stocking under the tree. When Mum said he really, really had to go to bed, he did, but he lay for a long time, listening. First, he heard Grandma coming upstairs and getting ready for bed. Then, he heard Mum. He heard her switch off the landing light and close her bedroom door, and it went dark, very dark. Her bed creaked, but at last it went quiet and he crept out of bed and pulled back the curtain.

The brightness took him by surprise. A full moon flooded his room with silvery light. Outside, the frost on the rooftops sparkled like snow, and the silence tingled as if a sleigh and a team of reindeer might appear at any moment. Quickly, he pinned a notice to his bedroom door:

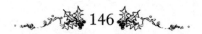

ABSOLOOTELY PRIVATE.
KEEP OUT.
If you have got any presents for me, please leave them downstairs.

Then he climbed onto a chair to put the Father Christmas Early Warning Device in place. Holding the bell clapper with one hand to keep it quiet, he used the other hand to fix one end of the elastic to the doorframe, and the other to the door with drawing pins, lots of drawing pins. Nails would have been better but he couldn't risk waking people by banging them in. When it all seemed secure he climbed down carefully, but left the chair in place as an extra obstacle. If Father Christmas tried to come in the bell would clang, and Timothy would wake up and shout for help. If Father Christmas still tried to push his way in, the chair would fall over and make more noise. Timothy told himself he was safe. There was no need to worry any more, but it still took him a long time to get to sleep. He heard

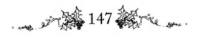

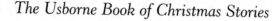

the clock in the hall strike eleven, and then half past eleven, then quarter to twelve. Soon after that he must have nodded off, because suddenly he realized he was awake – and the bell was jangling.

Timothy sat bolt upright, staring towards the door. The bell was clanging loudly but he couldn't see anything at all. What had happened to the silvery moon? Was this a nightmare?

Go... he tried to shout, but the "go" didn't come out, and the door was opening, opening…letting in a slit of light from the landing.

Jangle. It opened a bit more, casting a triangle of light onto the bedroom floor.

Jangle again. A bigger triangle – till something blocked it. Timothy sensed that somebody was there. He felt eyes staring at him, though he couldn't see a face.

Go away! The words still wouldn't come out. He willed the somebody to go away.

Jingle. Creak. Clatter.

The chair had fallen over.

"What the...?" said the somebody.

Timothy froze with fear, but at the same time he couldn't help thinking the voice sounded familiar. And there was something else, a familiar smell...of peppermint. A tremor of hope ran through him. Could it be? Was it?

The light went on. Timothy blinked, then closed his eyes to stop the glare. Then he opened them again very quickly because in the instant of a blink he'd glimpsed someone he thought he recognized. It was! It was his dad!

"Timbers." Dad always called him Timbers. "What's all this?" He was holding the bell clapper to stop it jangling. As fast as he could, Timothy jumped out of bed, ran to the door and hugged his big, lovely hairy-but-not-as-scary-as-Father-Christmas dad!

Then Mum appeared. "What's going on? What's all the noise?"

Timothy explained about the Early Warning Device. "I didn't want Father Christmas to come into my room, but it's a secret. Don't tell Lucy, please."

Dad carried Timothy back to bed. "Of course we won't tell her – or anyone. It's between you and me and Mum and Father Christmas. So you won't need this." Dad took down the Early Warning Device. "Mum and I know Father Christmas very well. He'll read your notice and leave your presents by the tree. He wants to make children happy, so he'll do exactly what you want."

"You and me and Mum and Father Christmas," said Timothy as he snuggled down to sleep. "That's okay."

And then, suddenly it seemed, it was morning. Timothy's bedroom door was bursting open and Lucy was whispering in his ear.

"He's been! He's been!" She was holding a bulging stocking. "Where's yours?"

"Downstairs in the sitting room."

"Let's go then." She headed downstairs.

Through the bedroom door on the other side of the

landing, Timothy could see his mum and dad. They looked as if they were fast asleep, but Mum lifted her head from the pillow to murmur sleepily, "Go down if you like, Tim. Open your stocking, but wait till we come before you open the tree presents."

Timothy's stocking lay under the tree, like a lumpy, well-fed snake. There was a note pinned to it:

Dear Tim,

I'll always leave your presents downstairs from now on.

Love F.C.

Soon, Mum and Dad and Gran came downstairs. Dad lit the fire. Mum switched on the Christmas-tree lights. Gran made tea and toast. Then they all opened their presents. Timothy got his favourite team's football kit, a

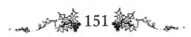

car track with two cars and a waterbomb pistol. Lucy gave him a Santa-in-a-box, which jumped out when he opened it – and Timothy laughed!

"Oh," said Lucy. "I thought you'd be scared."

But Timothy wasn't afraid of a tiny Father Christmas on a spring. He wasn't afraid of the real Father Christmas – not now. Father Christmas made children happy. Father Christmas was kind. He did what children wanted. He was *great*!

Billy's Christmas Surprises

Malcolm Yorke

Young Billy Reely-Dulle went downstairs to breakfast one morning in early December. It was always the same breakfast, a bowl of cornflakes, a cup of tea and a slice of toast. As usual his older sister Rosie was seated at the table and so was Mr. Reely-Dulle, doing exactly what they did every morning of the year.

Rosie was reading a book while she spooned in her cornflakes, because she never stopped reading books. She read at meals, in her bedroom, in the garden, in front of

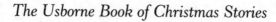

the TV and in the toilet. This might make her brilliant at school but it also made her pretty boring at home. Billy's father was hidden behind his newspaper reading all the financial stuff and underlining bits with his pen.

"Good morning, everybody," said Billy loudly and cheerfully. His father just rustled his newspaper, and Rosie glanced up from her book and nodded. From the next room Mrs. Reely-Dulle called, "Good morning, dear. Now please don't make any crumbs with that toast." She was polishing the potatoes and putting an extra shine on all the knives, forks and spoons. Already before breakfast she had ironed the newspapers, swept the pavement outside and made a list of twenty-seven jobs she had to do around the house during the day.

Billy sighed and ate his breakfast.

Before he had finished, his gran came downstairs.

"It's a bright frosty morning, Gran," Billy greeted her.

"Humph. Call this frost? When I was young we had *real* frost and when it was bright it was so bright you

154

couldn't see. Not like nowadays..." And she was off. Nothing was ever as good now as it had been in the old days and she told them so all day long. The weather, the food, the manners, and the clothes were all dreadful now compared to when she was young. "And as for that modern music, well, awful, shocking it is! Nothing like those good old tunes we used to dance to when I was a girl I can tell you!" But Billy had stopped listening ages ago.

It was like this every morning – boring, boring, boring. Billy used to ask his friends round to play sometimes but it was no fun. His sister went to her room to read, his father wrote his reports or added up rows of figures or whatever businessmen did, his gran moaned about today's young people and his mother fussed on about not making a mess or a noise or a spot of dirt. No wonder his friends never came back because, let's face it, he had the dullest family in the whole of this galaxy and probably the next one as well.

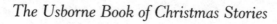

Mrs. Reely-Dulle collected the dishes and went to wash them twice over and then to launder the breakfast tablecloth as she did every morning. Her husband, dressed in his dark suit, dark tie, white shirt, black shoes and carrying his black umbrella and black briefcase set off to walk to the station to catch the 8.17 to the city. He worked on his financial papers all the way there and back and never spoke to anyone. Billy and Rosie set off for their different schools, Rosie reading as she walked, only looking up when she had to cross the road. Gran settled down to watch the TV all day, tut-tutting out loud about all the awful things people did and said these days, not like when she was young.

Billy soon met up with his friend Jacob who said, "Isn't it great Billy, only two weeks left until Christmas!"

"Yeah, I suppose so," replied Billy with no enthusiasm.

"What's wrong, don't you like Christmas?"

"I like the food and the carol singing and all that stuff, but I hate the presents bit."

"Hate presents! Are you daft! How can you hate presents?"

"Well, like everything our family does they're dead boring. I know now that Mum and Dad will give me new grey trousers, grey socks, grey shirt and a grey jumper. They'll just be one size bigger than last year's and the year's before and the year's before that."

"Is that all you'll get?"

"No, Rosie will give me a book and Gran some spending money and a sermon on how to spend it."

"You're dead right it *does* sound boring. So what'll you give them?"

"Well I'm so fed up I'm really going to give them a shock this year, do something special. So far though, I haven't had any bright ideas."

"What about money?"

"Not as big a problem as usual because I've saved hard all year, and then when my Aunty Mary won on the lottery she slipped me a few pounds."

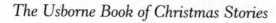
By this time they had arrived at school and soon they were kicking a ball around the playground before the bell went and lessons began.

Billy thought about Christmas again that evening as he watched Rosie read her book, his father work on his piles of papers, Gran watch TV and his mother vacuum the inside of the kitchen drawers. They were all nice people and he loved them dearly, but they did need a good shake-up.

He went to ask his mother, "Can I go shopping with Jacob and his mum this Saturday?"

"Of course, but remember to polish your shoes first dear, and take a clean handkerchief. Now pass me that doormat so I can give it a thorough scrub."

On Saturday morning Billy took his money along to the shopping centre and he and Jacob went looking for presents while Jacob's mum went round the supermarket.

"Let's start with Rosie," said Billy. "I'm willing to buy her anything except a book, she's already got thousands.

The problem is what? If you were her age, Jacob, what would you like somebody to give you?"

"Give me? No problem! A new pair of football boots."

"Right! Great idea and they might just get her away from reading for a bit." So Billy bought a pair her size, black with white flashes down the sides, and luminous yellow laces.

"Now what about my mum? It's got to be something she can't polish or dust."

"Difficult," admitted Jacob. "Does she like music? You can't dust that."

"I don't know – she's always too busy to stop and listen. But it's not a bad idea. What kind of music though? She'll never sit down long enough to listen to a concert."

"Well, a lot of people like dance music, don't they?"

"Okay, I'll get some of that. I notice they've got some CDs on special offer in the newsagent's. Now what about my dad? How can we liven him up?"

"That's a tough one," said Jacob, remembering how

serious Mr. Reely-Dulle always looked with his dark suits and his briefcase full of important papers. "I know, how about a coloured tie?"

"Good thinking, Jake! How about this purple one here with pink elephants all over it?"

"Yeah, that'll liven him up all right!"

So Billy bought it.

"Now we've got the biggest problem of all – Gran. She just watches telly all day and when we're home goes on and on and on about how everything was better years ago. Honestly, Jacob, she drives you round the bend."

"So what you need is something to put in her mouth so she can't talk."

"Hmm. Chocolates?"

"No. She'll finish them in a week. You also need to use up all that spare breath she's got."

By now they were standing outside a music shop with a window full of second-hand instruments.

"How about a trombone? No. Bagpipes? No. A trumpet?"

"I can't see your gran with a trumpet somehow, Billy, but what about this saxophone? It's on special offer and you get an instruction book free."

"Terrific!" So Billy bought the saxophone.

When they told Jacob's mum that Billy had bought football boots, dance music, a bright tie and a saxophone, she laughed and laughed. "Well they are in for a surprise at your house. I just hope they like them!" She knew Billy's family and she had her doubts.

At home Billy carefully wrapped the presents in Christmas paper and begged his mum not to look in his wardrobe – she was inclined to polish it inside and out every few days. As Christmas came nearer he began to wonder if he had bought the right presents. Would they really enjoy them?

On Christmas morning the family undid the presents under the tree. Billy was right: he did get new grey trousers, socks, shirt and jacket from his parents, and a book and spending money from Rosie and his gran. They had kept

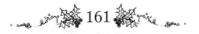

Billy's presents until last and now took turns to open them.

"Football boots!" said Rosie, astonished.

"Dance music!" exclaimed Mrs. Reely-Dulle, amazed.

"A funny tie!" said Mr. Reely-Dulle, flabbergasted.

Gran undid her parcel and was dumbfounded to find "A saxophone!"

They would never have chosen such weird things for themselves, but because they didn't want to hurt Billy's feelings they all thanked him very politely and tried to look enthusiastic. But privately they wondered whatever they would do with them.

On Boxing Day, Jacob came to call and the two boys insisted Rosie left her book, put her new boots on and come and kick a ball around with them. She reluctantly agreed. They showed her some tricky moves, how to pass and shoot and head, then they put her in goal and took penalties. Oddly enough she seemed to enjoy diving around in the mud and she brought off some spectacular saves.

"Hey, she's good," said Jacob to Billy when Rosie had

gone upstairs to scrape the muck off her knees and elbows and clothes. That afternoon they all three watched the big match on TV together.

"Now, this is fun," said Rosie. "Let's get Dad to take us all to the match tomorrow." After a bit of persuasion Mr. Reely-Dulle left his business accounts behind and found to his immense surprise that they all four enjoyed the game enormously.

Soon Mr. Reely-Dulle had to return to work after the Christmas holidays. He set off wearing his dark suit and white shirt, but just to please Billy he put on his brilliant new purple tie with the pink elephants.

Now usually all the businessmen travelled in absolute silence, each reading his newspaper, but this morning a man sitting opposite Mr. Reely-Dulle leaned forward and said, "I see from your tie you're the kind of chap who appreciates a joke. Have you heard the one about..." And then he told Billy's dad a very funny story. The other businessmen listened as well, from behind their

 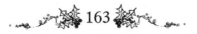

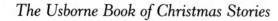

newspapers, and when Mr. Reely-Dulle guffawed they all joined in and had a good laugh too. Soon they were all swapping jokes and they kept it up all the way to the city. When Mr. Reely-Dulle walked into his office that morning even Miss Lemon his secretary smiled when she saw the tie, and so did all his colleagues and he smiled back. It was a good start to the New Year and Mr. Reely-Dulle thought he might try smiling a bit more often now he'd got the hang of it.

Back home Mrs. Reely-Dulle was dusting the ceilings with a long feather duster when she remembered her Christmas present. I'll give it a try, just to please Billy, she thought. She put the CD on and soon her toes began to twitch, then her feet tapped, then she did a twirl with the feather duster. Finally she gave up dusting, kicked off her shoes, and did a wild dance round the furniture. She danced until the music stopped, then played it right through again, and again. By the end of the afternoon she had not got through more than two of the things on her list

of twenty-seven household chores. And she didn't care!

Meanwhile Gran had gone off grumbling down to the garden shed. "That's not what I call dance music. Nothing like the proper tunes we had when I used to go to dances." She took her Christmas gift with her and the book of instructions. "I suppose young Billy meant well. It's a silly present but at least saxophones look the same as they did when I was young," she muttered.

First she tried a few tootles and honks and hoots. Then she soon got the hang of it and began to work her way through the instruction book. By the end of the afternoon she had mastered a tune and felt pretty pleased with herself. I wonder if there's anybody else who'd like to play the real old music, she thought as she went in for tea. She hadn't been near the TV all day.

Our story now jumps forward nearly a year and by then things were very different at the breakfast table of the Reely-Dulles. For a start they all sat down together and

talked about their exciting plans for the day or the weekend. From Monday to Friday Billy's dad now wore a blue or a green suit (and on hot summer days even a cream one) and had a whole collection of fancy ties. The purple one with the pink elephants was still his favourite though. He went off to work whistling and when he got on the 8.17 train all the businessmen there told jokes, played cards or dominoes and did crosswords together all the way into the city and all the way home. He made lots of new friends and he'd been promoted at work. On Saturday mornings he dressed in jeans and an old sweater because he ran a stall in the local market. He sold garden plants with his friend Patrick, the businessman who'd told him that first joke so long ago.

Mrs. Reely-Dulle hummed as she glided round the kitchen in her leotard and ankle warmers. After breakfast she would be off to her dance class. When Billy and Rosie were at school she rolled back the carpets and danced and leaped and cavorted and twirled all over the house. She'd

bought a lot more tapes and CDs now but the one Billy had given her was still the one she played most.

When Mr. Reely-Dulle came home he danced with her, and on Friday evenings they both went off to the disco – they had even won prizes for their dance routines! The house was pretty untidy these days because she was so busy practising – "But who cares?" said Mrs. Reely-Dulle with a laugh.

Gran usually finished her breakfast and hurried off to the garden shed to turn the heating on before the rest of her band arrived. She had recruited a gang of other lively pensioners who played waltzes, quicksteps, tangos and foxtrots and other old-time songs and dances ("They don't write music like that any more," she said). They called themselves The Wrinkly Swingers and played at socials, fêtes, weddings and Bar Mitzvahs. They'd even been on local radio. The drummer, Arthur, used to be a bandsman in the army and he was terrific, a real star. Billy suspected he might fancy Gran because he came round to

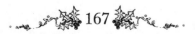

rehearse in the garden shed more often than the others and took her out for a drink afterwards. "I think we'll make a record soon," Gran told Billy one morning. "Then we can go on *Top of the Pops* and show you youngsters what good music is really like."

As Billy finished his breakfast this Saturday morning just before Christmas, he could hear lots of Rosie's friends pounding up the stairs to her room. She was the goalkeeper and captain of the local girls' team (they had already beaten several boys' sides and were third in the league). They plotted tactics on the blackboard in her room ready for the afternoon's match. She was still brilliant at school and loved books, but at least now she knew how to have some fun with other people. Most evenings Billy and Jacob gave her penalties practice in the back garden.

Billy sat alone at the table, surrounded by crumbs and dirty dishes. Now his mum didn't bother so much, Billy would have to clear them up himself, but he didn't mind. He could hear disco music from the front room where his

mum was jiving, a slow waltz from down the garden shed
where Gran was doing a solo on the saxophone, his father
laughing and telling jokes while he and his friend Patrick
loaded up trays of plants in the garage, and shrill girls'
voices arguing about whether or not to use a three-four-
three formation came from up above. Soon Jacob and a
dozen of Billy's own friends would be round to play and
make a lot more noise and mess.

Just sometimes it might be nice to have a bit of peace
and quiet like before, thought Billy. But no, this family
could never again be as dull and boring as they were
before he gave them their last year's Christmas presents.
He smiled when he remembered the changes those odd
gifts had caused – it just showed what magic was in the
air at Christmas.

He was pretty sure he wouldn't be getting any drab
grey clothes this year, because he'd taught the others
what fun presents could be. His only problem now was
whatever could he give them this Christmas?

Sparrow's Special Christmas

Susan Gates

I'm in a really bad mood! Christmas is cancelled. There isn't going to be a Christmas this year.

We're snowed in! When I woke up this morning the whole world was white. We couldn't believe it. Even the weather girl on telly couldn't believe it: "It really took us by surprise," she said.

"I hate you, snow!" I told it. I even shook my fist out of the window at it.

Tomorrow is *supposed* to be Christmas Day. But we haven't got any crackers or Christmas pudding yet. And we haven't got my new bike! Dad was *supposed* to be collecting it from the town today. But now he can't get through to the shops. Not even on the tractor. We've got to wait for the snow ploughs to dig us out.

I asked Mum, "Why do you always have to leave things until the last minute? Why didn't you get my bike before?"

And Mum said, "Because we're so busy. There's so much to do on the farm."

They're always busy. Feeding the sheep, fixing fences, doing all sorts of jobs. They're out there now, seeing if the sheep are all right. They don't have time for Christmas.

And I'm stuck here with Gran. She always comes to our house for Christmas.

"Lucky I got here before the snow," she says. "Or I wouldn't have got here at all."

I just grunt, "*Harumph!*" I'm in such a bad mood. Bet

all my friends are having a *proper* Christmas. Bet *their* mums and dads did the shopping on time.

Crash! The front door bursts open. Mum staggers in. She looks like an Arctic explorer, all crusty with snow. Her eyelashes are frozen! They look like they're threaded with little glass beads.

"*Burrr*," she says, pulling off her boots. "It's dreadful out there!"

"You mean you can't get to the shops?" I ask her.

"We were lucky to get to the top field," she says. "It's really, really bad. Your dad's trying to get the sheep in now."

Gran says, "I haven't seen a Christmas like this since 1947. In 1947 me and your grandad had Fold House Farm. And we were snowed up there. We had to warm the Christmas lambs up in the bottom of the big oven. It was the only way to keep them alive."

I give a big yawn. I know it's rude but I can't help it. I've heard this story before — about warming the Christmas lambs in the big oven. We don't do that kind of thing nowadays. We've got special incubator things to warm up Christmas lambs. They work with electricity.

Mum says: "It's getting worse out there!"

"Oh no!" I say. "What a horrible, horrible Christmas. Didn't you even get me some sweets – a selection box or something?"

"No," says my mum. "We were going to do most of our Christmas shopping today. We were even going to collect the turkey today. I'm really, really sorry, Sparrow."

My mum and dad always call me Sparrow. It's not my real name of course. Katherine's my real name.

"Look, Sparrow," says Mum, suddenly. "I've got something to show you."

Maybe she did get a present after all!

But it isn't a present. It's a catalogue. Mum opens it and says, "There's the bike we've got you, Sparrow. I know it's not the same as your real present. But at least you can look at a picture of it."

I'm so mad, I refuse to look at the picture.

"What kind of a Christmas present is that?" I shout at Mum. "A stupid picture? I can't ride around on a picture, can I? I want my proper Christmas present! Not just a stupid picture!"

And do you know what I do next? Throw the catalogue in the waste-paper bin, that's what I do. I know I'm acting like a little kid. But I just can't help it. Christmas should be really nice. Christmas should be just perfect.

"At least you've got a Christmas tree," says Gran. "Look how pretty the lights are."

Then guess what happens? The Christmas-tree lights go out.

I can't believe it! One second they're bright and twinkly. The next they're dead.

"Oh, no," sighs Mum. "Not a power cut! The snow must have brought the wires down."

That's all I need. No presents, no sweets, no turkey. And now no Christmas television. This is going to be the worst Christmas ever!

***

It's Christmas morning. When I wake up the first thing I do is shiver, *"Burrr!"* There's still no electricity. My radiator is freezing cold. When I breathe out, *"Huuuhh!"* my breath makes little white clouds.

There's a bright white light coming through my curtains. I know what that means. It means the snow's still there. Last night I dreamed it had all melted away. And my dad got through to town – five minutes before the bike shop closed. And when I went downstairs on Christmas morning there was a bike-shaped parcel, under the Christmas tree.

Who am I kidding? When I look outside the snow is worse than ever.

"I hate you, snow!" I say, out loud. I make a hideous face at it, through the window.

Might as well stay in bed. There's nothing to get up for. I'm just snuggling back into my duvet when Gran calls from downstairs.

"Katherine, are you awake?"

Gran never calls me Sparrow, she always calls me Katherine.

Her voice sounds a bit worried so I wrap myself in my duvet and get out of bed.

"Ow!" The floor's icy cold.

"Ow!" I've just fallen over my shepherd's crook. It's the one I had for the school Christmas play. Every year I'm a shepherd! Just because I live on a farm. I'm sick of it. Why can't I be an angel for a change? Why can't I have big, silver wings?

I drag myself downstairs in my duvet. Gran's in the kitchen lighting a fire in the old fireplace.

"Pet Sheep hasn't come to the kitchen door," she says.

I haven't told you about Pet Sheep. Sometimes, on the farm, we get a lamb whose mother dies or is too sick to feed it. So we feed the lamb with a bottle. And it gets really tame and it gets used to us. And we call it our Pet Lamb. And when it grows up we call it our Pet Sheep. We've got a Pet Sheep now and she's always hanging round the kitchen door. She lives in the little paddock by the barn. And she comes to the back door for food. She likes Polo mints but don't tell Mum I feed her those. Today, because it's Christmas Day, I was going to give her a whole tube of Polo mints for a present. They're on the mantelpiece, wrapped in silver foil, all ready for her. But she hasn't come to get them.

"Where are Mum and Dad?" I ask Gran. "Have you told them about Pet Sheep?"

"They're digging out sheep in the top field," says Gran. "I hope they're all right. This snow is really bad."

I forget about feeling grumpy. Suddenly, there's a sick, shivery feeling inside my stomach.

"They will be all right, won't they, Gran?" I ask her.

Gran doesn't answer my question. Her face looks grim and serious. She just says, "Katherine, I haven't seen a Christmas as bad as this since 1947."

It doesn't feel like Christmas. Christmas should be

warm and bright and sparkly. But our house is cold and gloomy. And I'm worried about Pet Sheep and worried about Mum and Dad, out there in the snowdrifts.

Then I remember something else that makes me even more worried.

"Pet Sheep is going to lamb soon," I tell Gran. "But it's not until next week."

"You sometimes get early lambs," says Gran. "Sometimes they come when you don't expect them."

"Don't say that, Gran. She can't have her lamb now. Not in all this snow!"

The paddock is only across the farmyard. You can see it from the back door. But the farmyard is full of deep, deep snow. It's as high as our kitchen windows.

"We must get to Pet Sheep," I tell Gran desperately. "She might need our help!"

Then Gran starts one of her stories. I can't believe it! This is an emergency! Pet Sheep might be buried under a snowdrift. She might be having an early lamb. All on her own, in this weather. And my Grandma's telling stories about olden times!

"In 1947," says Gran, "in that bad winter, our sheep got buried under snowdrifts. And I was really skinny then, just like I am now. I didn't weigh much at all. Your grandad said I was light as a feather. And do you know, if you don't weigh much you can walk on snowdrifts, you don't sink in."

I was going to yawn. But I stop myself, just in time. And I start listening to Gran's story. I mean, *really* listening.

"I went out to find the sheep," Gran tells me. "I walked on top of the snowdrifts. I had a long stick and every three steps I poked it into the snow to see if a sheep was buried."

"How did you know when you'd found one?" I ask her.

"They wriggle," says Gran. "When you poke them with a stick, they wriggle, under the snow."

Why didn't I think of that? I'm getting excited now.

"I could walk on the snowdrifts," I tell Gran. "I could

do that! I don't weigh much. That's why my dad calls me Sparrow."

"You're not going," says Gran sternly. "If anyone's going, I'm going!"

"I'm coming too. It's my Pet Sheep!"

Gran frowns.

"I'm lighter than you!" I tell her.

"All right," says Gran. "You can come. At least I can keep an eye on you."

I throw off my duvet: "Let's get ready then!"

We get ready in double-quick time. Socks, jumpers, trousers, wellies, gloves, hats. We look like big, fat caterpillars when we've finished.

"And now," says Gran, "we need a long stick."

We look round the kitchen.

"I know!" I tell Gran. "I know what we'll use!"

I clump upstairs in my wellies and grab my shepherd's crook. You know, I'm glad now I wasn't an angel this year. I clump downstairs again.

"Perfect," says Gran when she sees my crook. "That's just what we need."

"Wait," I tell Gran. I clump over to the mantelpiece. Pet Sheep's Christmas present is there – the tube of Polo mints, all wrapped up. I stick it in my coat pocket.

Gran picks up a spade from beside the kitchen door. "We might need this," she says.

We're ready now. Ready to go on a rescue mission to find Pet Sheep!

"I'll test the snow first," says Gran.

And then she does this amazing thing! She opens the kitchen window. She climbs up on to the sofa. And she walks out of the window. She walks right out onto the snow! Just like that!

She bounces up and down on it, as if it's a trampoline! It goes, squeak, squeak, under her wellies. But she doesn't sink in.

"It's nice and firm," says Gran. "You can come out now."

So I climb out of the window too.

And we're walking on top of snowdrifts, me and Gran! The snow's crunchy and creaky but we don't sink. The sun comes out and makes the snow bright and sparkly. And it's really Christmassy. It's brilliant. It's like walking on top of a giant Christmas cake!

But then I start worrying about Pet Sheep.

I'm getting cold now. *Clack, clack, clack.* What's that noise? It's my teeth.

"Here's the paddock, Gran!"

We nearly missed it. Because all you can see is the top of the paddock wall, poking above the snow.

"Start sliding the crook in," says Gran. "Gently, gently," she warns. "And try close to the wall. That's where sheep like to shelter."

I slide in my shepherd's crook. Did something wriggle? Or is it me shivering?

"No," says Gran. She's listening hard. Listening for scuffling sounds deep under the snow. "Nothing there. Try this place here."

We try and try. We scrunch round the paddock. And every three steps we poke another hole. But we don't find anything. Nothing wriggles under the snow.

I'm so cold and tired I'm nearly crying. The sun has gone in. "More snow on the way," says Gran, looking at the grey clouds.

"We'll never find Pet Sheep!" I say.

And I nearly give up. But my little gran doesn't give up. She doesn't seem to feel the cold. She's tough, my gran. She can chuck hay bales about. I've seen her. Not many grans can do that.

"Let's try over there," she says.

I trudge after her. I've got three pairs of socks on but my toes are like ice-pops. I've got gloves on but my fingers are stinging like mad and I want to go back and...

Whoops! I've tripped over something. I crash to my knees and my hand reaches out and grabs something: "Urgh, what's that?" It's wool, all crispy with ice.

"Pet Sheep!" I cry. "It's Pet Sheep!"

Pet Sheep isn't buried very deep. I start digging like mad with my hands like a dog digging up a bone. There's snow flying all around. But Gran gently pushes me out the way. I forgot she'd brought a spade.

Very carefully, she starts to dig. And soon I see Pet Sheep's head.

"She's all right. Look, she's all right."

"Baaa!" says Pet Sheep.

"Come with us, girl," I tell Pet Sheep. "You're only a little sheep. You can walk on the snow too."

But Pet Sheep doesn't move. She doesn't wriggle free. She just stays in her hole in the snow.

I unwrap her Christmas present. "Come on girl, come on!" I hold out a Polo. But even a Polo mint won't make her follow me.

"I think I know what's wrong," says Gran.

Gently, very gently, she clears more snow away. She does it with her hands, not the spade. And she finds a soggy little bundle.

I peer into the hole in the snow: "It's a lamb!"

"She won't come without her lamb," says Gran.

Gran lifts out the lamb and it's floppy. Its legs are all dangly.

"Is it dead?" I ask her.

"Nearly," says Gran. "We'd better hurry back."

As fast as we can, we start plodding back to the house. I carry the crook and the spade. Gran hugs the lamb to her coat. Pet Sheep scrambles out of the hole and comes trotting after us.

It's starting to snow again. Big soft flakes that stick to your face.

"Hurry!" says Gran, urgently.

I can't see where we're going. The world is all white and whirling. But Gran knows the way. And soon we're crawling back through the kitchen window.

"What about Pet Sheep?"

Pet Sheep pokes her head through the window: "Baaaa!"

"Leave her outside," says Gran. "We'll see to her in a minute. It's her lamb I'm worried about."

The lamb's eyes are closed.

"We'll have to warm it up," says Gran.

"I'll get the incubator!" I go racing off. I know where it is. It's in the storeroom, under the stairs.

Then I remember, "Oh no!"

There's no electricity.

Gran takes the lamb close to the fire. But it still looks dead. "Poor little mite," says Gran.

I nearly ask: "What did you do in 1947, Gran?" But then I remember. They warmed lambs up in the bottom of the big oven. And guess what? Our oven's electric.

But my gran isn't beaten yet.

"Have you got any baking foil?" she asks me. "You know, the silver kind, that comes on a roll?"

"Yes, we have!"

I know we have because my mum's got some extra-wide foil for the Christmas turkey. But we couldn't collect the turkey so we don't need it any more, do we?

I grab the foil from a cupboard and Gran tears off a big piece. Then she wraps the lamb in it!

"That'll keep it warm," she says.

My gran's a genius. She really is.

"Have you got a cardboard box?"

"There's the box that we keep the Christmas tree decorations in."

"That'll do."

So we put the lamb in the box. It looks like a Christmas present, all done up in silver wrapping. We put the box by the fire. Then we sit and wait.

"Baa!" goes Pet Sheep outside the window. She's worried about her baby.

"It's all right, Pet Sheep!" I call out to her in a cheerful voice. "You can have your baby back in a minute. But we've got to warm it up first!"

But I don't feel cheerful. The lamb isn't moving at all.

"Please let it be alive!" I wish. "Please let it be alive.

It'd be the best Christmas present ever!"

But the lamb still doesn't move.

Gran shakes her head. "It's been out in the cold too long," she says, sadly.

I feel really sad too. As if there's a heavy stone inside me. I get up from the fire. I drag myself over to the window one...step...at...a...time. I don't want to do it. But I've got to. I've got to tell Pet Sheep what's happened.

"Hang on a minute," says Gran.

She peers into the box. I rush back and peer into the box too.

The silver foil's going all crinkly, as if there's something twitching inside it.

"Maaa!" says the lamb, in a tiny voice. "Maaa!"

The front door crashes open. A gust of snow blows in. And there are Mum and Dad. They've come back safe from the snowdrifts! They're stomping around to keep warm. Slapping the snow off their clothes.

"Are you all right, Sparrow?" asks Dad.

"Dad! We've rescued Pet Sheep. Me and Gran did it. We walked on the snowdrifts. We dug her out. She's got a lamb! And look, it's still alive!"

I'm in bed, wrapped in my duvet. I'm warm because I've got two hot-water bottles. Christmas Day is nearly over.

What a funny Christmas Day! It wasn't a proper Christmas. We didn't have crackers or turkey or a selection box. We ate soup warmed up on the fire. Then we warmed up tinned rice pudding for afters.

But Pet Sheep's lamb grew stronger and stronger. She was going, "MAAA! MAAA!" while we ate our Christmas dinner. She was standing up on wobbly legs. As soon as we knew she was all right we gave her back to Pet Sheep. They're out in the barn, with lots of hay to keep them warm. So I've got a Pet Sheep and Pet Lamb now. Wonder if Pet Lamb likes Polos as much as her mum?

You know that catalogue that I threw away? With the picture of my Christmas bike in it? Well, I went to get it out of the waste-paper bin. It was all crumpled up so I smoothed it out. And do you know what? It's a beautiful silver bike. I can't wait to get it. I've cut the picture out and put it under my pillow. But I keep taking it out and putting my torch on so I can have another look.

It wasn't a *proper* Christmas. But it was a special Christmas. I'll never forget it. And when I get really old, like Gran, I'll tell everyone about it. About the special Christmas when we had soup for our Christmas dinner. When Gran and me walked on snowdrifts and dug out Pet Sheep. And saved Pet Lamb's life by wrapping her in silver foil that was meant for the Christmas turkey!

Baboushka

Alice Low

It was the night that Jesus was born in Bethlehem. In a faraway country an old woman named Baboushka sat in her snug little house by her warm fire. The wind was drifting the snow outside and howling down the chimney, but it only made Baboushka's fire burn more brightly.

"How glad I am to be indoors," said Baboushka, holding out her hands to the bright blaze.

Suddenly she heard a loud rap at her door. She opened it and there stood three splendidly dressed old men. Their beards were as white as the snow, and so long they almost reached the ground. Their eyes shone kindly in the light of Baboushka's candle, and their arms were full of precious things – boxes of jewels and sweet-smelling oils and ointments.

"We have travelled far, Baboushka," they said, "and we have stopped to tell you of the babe born this night in Bethlehem. He has come to rule the world and teach us to be loving and true. We are bringing Him gifts. Come with us, Baboushka."

Baboushka looked at the swirling, drifting snow and then inside at her cosy room and the crackling fire. "It is too late for me to go with you, good sirs," she said. "The night is too cold." She shut the door and went inside, and the old men journeyed to Bethlehem without her.

But as Baboushka sat rocking by her fire, she began to think about the baby Prince, for she loved babies.

"Tomorrow I will go to find Him," she said, "tomorrow, when it is light, and I will carry Him some toys."

In the morning Baboushka put on her long cloak and took her staff, and she filled her basket with the pretty things a baby would like – gold balls and wooden toys and strings of silver cobwebs – and she set out to find the baby.

But Baboushka had forgotten to ask the three old men the way to Bethlehem, and they had travelled so far during the night that she could not catch up with them. Up and down the road she hurried, through woods and fields and towns, telling everyone she met, "I am looking for the baby Prince. Where does He lie? I have some pretty toys for Him."

But no one could tell her the way. "Farther on, Baboushka, farther on," was their only reply. So she travelled on and on and on for years and years – but she never found the little Prince.

They say that Baboushka is travelling still, looking for Him. And every year, when Christmas Eve comes and all the children are lying fast asleep, Baboushka trudges softly through the snowy fields and towns, wrapped in her long cloak and carrying her basket on her arm. Gently she raps at every door.

"Is He here?" she asks. "Is the baby Prince here?" But the answer is always no, and sorrowfully she starts on her way again. Before she leaves, though, she lays a toy from her basket beside the pillow of each child. "For His sake," she says softly, and then hurries on through the years, for ever in search of the baby Prince.

Houston Calling
Chris d'Lacey

Once there was a boy called Willie Blastov who lived on a farm in the far north of Russia. Willie didn't have any brothers or sisters, and his mother had died when he was three. Boris, Willie's father, was a good, kind man. He loved his son dearly and taught him all the ways of farming. He taught Willie how to tend a herd of goats, and plant turnips in lines, and when to expect the rain to fall. Willie listened well and worked hard for his father, even in the driving cold of winter. This pleased

195

Farmer Blastov to the toes of his boots, but it troubled him greatly too. Willie was such a good little boy. Many times Boris wished he could reward him with a present. But how could a poor man afford to buy presents when every last scrap of money must be spent on the farm?

At Christmas, this feeling always grew worse. Every year on Christmas Eve, when Willie was tucked up snugly in bed, Boris would sit in his creaky old rocking chair, watching snowflakes patter against the farmhouse windows, thinking of the other boys around the world waking in the morning to presents from Santa. It was terrible. All he could manage to give his boy was a small bag of nuts or an orange perhaps – and only then in a year when the turnip harvest had been at its very best.

Then, one Christmas, an idea struck him. An idea so perfectly, wonderfully simple that he wondered if his brain had not been stuffed with straw all these years. Leaping up from his chair, he opened a notepad on the kitchen table. Then he sat down and wrote out a letter.

To Santa Claus. It went like this:

> Dear Mr. Santa Claus,
>
> If you are passing this way on Christmas night, please will you bring my son, Willie, a present? He is a good, honest boy. He helps on the farm and never complains, even when the cold is chewing his bones. I want to give him a special present. But the crops have been very poor this year and I do not have any money to spare. Willie likes animals. He also likes to stare at the stars. Please help, if you can.
>
> Your friend, Farmer Blastov

Farmer Blastov folded the note and threw it up the farmhouse chimney. The wind caught the paper and carried it away. Away across the barren lands to the north. Away beyond the frosty, frozen tundra. Away across the icy Arctic Ocean. Until...*plop!* It fluttered down another large chimney, a chimney on top of a tiny wooden

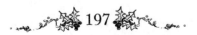

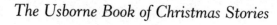

workshop, somewhere close to the North Pole itself.

That dark and peaceful Christmas night, while Willie was fast asleep, dreaming of reindeer, Santa Claus came and visited the farm. He took Farmer Blastov's note from his pocket. A special present? For a good, honest boy? One who likes animals and staring at stars? Santa thought hard. He stroked his beard. He didn't know what he could give such a boy. Then an elf whispered something into his ear. The bells on Santa's hat began to jangle. Ah yes. Of course. He rummaged in a dark, fluffy corner of his sack. And with a huff and a tug, he brought out a bear.

It was a perfectly ordinary brown teddy bear. It had big, round ears and a good-sized snout and nice, smooth pads on its sticky-out paws. On its body it wore a vest. A black woolly vest, as black as space. Rockets and stars were sewn onto the front, and right across the back was a fiery comet.

Santa sat the bear in the palm of his hand. "You are a special bear," he said. "Wherever Willie goes, you go too."

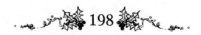

Then he placed the bear on Willie's pillow. And in a twinkle of Christmas dust, he was gone.

In the morning, Willie was so excited that he woke his father before the sun rose. He had always wanted to own a bear. And now he had one with *stars* on its vest! Hugging the bear up under his chin, Willie said to his father, "Father, look what Santa has brought me! I shall love this bear for ever and ever and take him everywhere I go..."

And he did. He took the bear down to the stream in the valley. He took him to the hen house and let him gather eggs. He even let him ride on the back of a goat. But their favourite place was the top of the hill. From here they could watch the reindeer herds, moving like clouds across the far horizon. And when the sun went down and the pale moon rose, they could gaze at the distant, winking stars.

Willie had always loved the stars. At night, he dreamed of flying to the moon in a silver rocket with big

blue fins. He dreamed about floating in outer space, too. And walking on the moon. And wearing a space-suit. He dreamed of these things for years and years – until there came a time to dream no more...

...for in time, Willie Blastov grew to be a man. An important man. A famous man. At the age of twelve he had said goodbye to his father's farm and gone to the city to learn about space. By the age of twenty he could fly a jet plane. Five years later he could fly a rocket. By the time his thirtieth birthday had arrived he had circled the moon and touched the stars. Now, at the age of thirty-two, he was the finest cosmonaut in the whole of Russia.

Yet, despite his fame and high importance, he never forgot his gift from Santa. By now the bear was a raggy old thing, loved so much that his fur was thinning and his seams were popping and his snout was almost worn away. But for all that he had lost, he had gained something too. And that something was a rather unusual name. In the early years on the farm, Willie had struggled to think of a

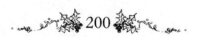

name he could give his bear. Many had he tried; none
seemed to fit. Then one day his Great Aunt Misha
had visited from Moscow. Aunt Misha had been on a
holiday to America, to a well-known city in Texas, called
Houston. Here, she told Willie, was the place from
which the American astronauts guided the launching of
all their rockets.

"They call it 'Mission Control'," she had beamed.

These words had stuck in Willie's mind. They stuck
so hard that he thought at first he would call his new
friend "Mission Control". But it seemed such a long and
clumsy name. So plain old "Houston" the bear became.

Now, whenever Willie left to go on a mission, he would
cuddle Houston close and place him on the bedroom
windowsill. There, with the moon in his glassy-eyed
gaze, the bear would sit and watch the skies, waiting for
Willie's return.

And in space, Willie Blastov would think about

Houston. He would stare at the vast and beautiful earth and see Russia like a piece of a jigsaw puzzle. And he knew that within that puzzle was a town, and in that town a house, a house with a bear in a bedroom window. It always sent a frown across Willie's face. For he would think about the promise he had made to his father so long ago when he lived on the farm: *I shall love this bear for ever and ever and take him everywhere I go...* If only he could bring little Houston up here. On just one mission. Just one. Once.

It happened on Willie's thirty-third birthday. Instead of sitting Houston in the window as usual, Willie slipped him neatly inside his jacket. When he boarded his rocket, not even the man with the TV camera noticed the furry ear just flopping out of the cosmonaut's spacesuit. Houston had made it into a rocket. He was about to be the first bear in space.

When the rocket blasted off it nearly took Houston's ears off! All his stuffing seemed to sink into his legs.

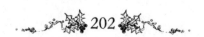

There was a frightening boom when the rocket burst out of the atmosphere, too. But the booms and rattles soon settled down and before long the rocket nosed into the darkness and hardly seemed to be moving at all.

Now, one bright morning, while Houston was floating near the spaceship window, watching the glittering stars go by, a fascinating object appeared in the sky. It looked a bit like a miniature spacecraft. There were dishes and fins and long antennae poking out from it in all directions. It was a television satellite called TV1. It was broken and Willie needed to repair it. There was only one way to reach the satellite. Willie had to leave the ship and walk in space.

Quickly, he put on his suit and helmet, and clipped a long, strong cord to a belt on his waist. The other end he clipped to a part of the spaceship. "This is so I don't drift away," he told Houston. Then he reached down into a pocket of his spacesuit and brought out another, shorter cord. "And this," he said, with a moon-sized grin, "is so

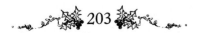

you don't drift away, old friend!" And he clipped the short cord to his belt as well and tried to fix the other end to Houston's paw...

...except the clip wouldn't stay on the paw very well. So Willie fastened it to Houston's ear instead. He tugged it gently to check that it was safe. The clip held firm. It would not come off. Willie pushed a few buttons. The spacecraft door slid silently open. Holding Houston tight to his chest, Willie stepped out into space.

It was a giant leap for bearkind everywhere. Never before had a man and his teddy floated above the beautiful blue earth. Willie thought his heart would surely burst. He remembered back to that first Christmas morning when the bright-eyed bear in the black rocket-vest had turned up on his pillow. How could he have guessed that one day they would be walking together in space? He brought Houston up to the glass of his helmet. "I told you I would take you everywhere," he said, "and now you can see what space is *really* like!" Carefully, Willie opened his hands. Houston

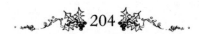

floated away, but only as far as his cord would allow. He bobbed slightly and tilted back. His beaming face seemed to light up the sky.

With a smile, Willie turned to the broken satellite. After an hour of unbolting panels and testing circuits and adjusting screws, the fault on TV1 was repaired. Willie glanced across at Houston. The bear had come to rest in the far receiving dish. "All done," Willie told him, and turned to reel the old bear in. And it was then that disaster struck. Suddenly, Houston's cord went taut. It had snagged on a fin of TV1. Willie pulled without thinking. In the silent vacuum of outer space there was a less-than-silent tearing sound. It was a floppy ear detaching from a teddy bear's head...

"HOUSTON!!!" Willie screamed.

But it was all too late. The last strands of cotton worked out of the seam and Houston went tumbling into the darkness. Willie stretched his silver-gloved hands into the emptiness, but all that came back to him was one

raggy ear on the end of a cord. Houston, the faithful teddy, was gone. Lost in the cold, deep well of space.

Back on earth, Willie Blastov was welcomed home as a hero. But when the press came to learn of the terrible tragedy, pictures of Houston and his famous companion were flashed up on television screens the world over. All that week, newspapers printed dramatic tales of Houston's life, from plain farm bear to first bear in space. They called him a pioneer; a great explorer. One paper produced a medal in his honour.

But for Willie, many fretful months went by. Comforting letters flooded into his home from every country across the globe. Bears were sent too, lots of bears, but none could replace a friend like Houston. And so, as Christmas came around, Willie gave all the bears away and decided he would go back home for a while, to spend some days on his father's farm.

It was there on the farm, two days before the eve of

Christmas, that something rather peculiar happened. Willie and his father had just settled down to watch a football match on Russian television when – *fzzt! zzipp!* – the screen went fuzzy. Farmer Blastov muttered in annoyance, got up and banged the top of the set. The picture came back. Then it went off again. All over Russia, people fiddled and banged and shouted at their televisions. It made no difference. The problem was not with the sets at all. The problem was with the signal. TV1 had broken down again. This was a very serious business. If TV1 was not repaired quickly everyone in Russia would miss the Christmas ice hockey final! But what had made the satellite faulty again? And why was it bleeping strange signals to earth? Scientists at the space centre scratched their heads. They checked their computers. They double-checked their computers. *Interference*, the computers reported.

"Interference?" the scientists muttered. Interference from what? And then one scientist whispered to another,

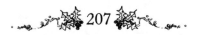

"Perhaps it's Commander Blastov's bear!"

It was supposed to be a joke – but before long the joke was a serious rumour. Within hours, the rumour was a newspaper headline...

"HOUSTON CALLING!" the papers cried.
"BLASTOV'S BEAR COMES BOUNCING BACK!"

And wonderful theories began to emerge of how Houston might have orbited the earth and somehow landed back on TV1. Scientists scoffed at the very idea. But a young astronomer in Northern Italy claimed he had seen, through a high-powered telescope, a brown furry object clinging to the satellite and knocking its paw on the far receiving dish! The earth buzzed with expectation. Was it *really* Commander Blastov's bear? And if so...could the bear be saved?

Willie Blastov shook his head in despair. He knew very

well that rockets cost a great deal of money to launch. And to launch a mission to rescue a *bear*? That was far too much to ask. "Even if they tried," he told his father, "in the time it would take to reach the satellite, Houston could just as easily have drifted off into space again."

Farmer Blastov grunted kindly and rested a notepad on his knee. For the last ten minutes he'd been sitting in his rocking chair, quietly composing a handwritten letter. He stood up and walked to the open fire. "That bear is a special bear," he said. "If there is a way back, he will find it." And to Willie's astonishment, Farmer Blastov bent forward and threw his letter up the chimney.

"Father, why did you do that?" asked Willie.

Farmer Blastov glanced through the misted windows. Snow was falling over the farm. "Just an old man's superstitious folly," he said. And he drank down a very small glass of vodka, and went off to bed.

The earth seemed very silent as Christmas approached.

But in every country, in every town, prayers were being said for the little bear, Houston. On Christmas Eve, Willie Blastov said a prayer too. He lay in the bed he had slept in as a boy and rubbed Houston's ear between his thumb and fingers. Tomorrow, he told himself, on Christmas Day morning, he would go to the top of the highest hill, where he and Houston had marvelled at the stars so many times, and there he would scrape a hole in the ground. He would bury the fragment of the bear inside it, and hope to bury his sorrow as well. The clock at the side of the bed chimed twelve. "Goodnight, Houston, wherever you are," said Willie, and he fell into a deep and shuddering sleep.

Darkness surrounded the tiny farmhouse. Snowflakes pattered on the window panes. In the room next to Willie's, Farmer Blastov snored. The clock chimed four. A pine needle fell off the Christmas tree. The fire died out. The wind howled softly...

...and something bright flashed across the sky.

In the room where Willie Blastov slept, there was a sudden icy swirl of wind.

"Ah, yes. I remember this place," said a voice. It was Santa Claus. He had a note in his hand. He blew the fresh soot off the words and read:

Dear Mr. Santa Claus,

Many years ago, you brought my boy a bear. A small brown bear with a starry black vest. I asked for this gift because my son had always worked hard on the farm. He is a man, now, but he has continued to work hard all his life. He has travelled to the stars and back again. His work has made many people happy. But he is now very, very unhappy. It was there, among the stars, that he lost his bear. He cares for it very much indeed. It is old now, and ragged, and it only has one ear. But it has all the love of the world inside it. Please help my boy to find it if you can. You are his last hope.

Your friend, Farmer Blastov

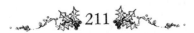

Santa Claus stroked his beard in thought. A small brown bear with only one ear? Now where had he seen one just like that?

"In space, of course," a clever elf said.

Santa frowned. The bells on his hat began to jangle. Oh yes, *that* bear. That nuisance he had picked off the satellite dish. The one that was knocking its paw on the dish and causing interference to the TV pictures – just when everyone at the North Pole was looking forward to the Christmas ice hockey final! They could certainly have *that* bear back. Santa rummaged in the bottom of his sack. "I think the farmer means you," he said to a bear with a tattered rocket-vest and a few loose stitches in one side of its head.

An elf fetched the ear off Willie's pillow. Santa held it against the bear's head.

"It fits," said the elf, and in a twinkle of stardust the ear was stitched.

Santa put the bear on Willie's pillow. "Love this bear

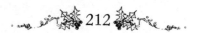

for ever," he whispered. "And NEVER let go of him in

space again!"

"I won't," Willie Blastov mumbled, sleepily. He put
out an arm and cuddled the old bear into his body.

Santa smiled and picked up his sack. "Next house," he
boomed.

And with a jingle of bells his sledge was gone.

And Houston, the first bear in space, was home.

Cobweb Christmas

Shirley Climo

Once upon a Christmastime, long ago in
Germany, there lived a little old woman. She
was so little she had to climb upon a step stool
to reach her feather bed and so old she could-
n't even count all the Christmases she'd seen.
The children in her village called her Tante,
which means "Auntie" in German.

Tante's home was a cottage at the edge of a
thick fir forest. The cottage had but one room,
one door, and one window, and no upstairs to
it at all. It suited the old woman, for there was
room enough within its walls for her to keep a
canary for singing, a cat for purring, and a dog
to doze beside the fire.

Squeezed up against the cottage was a

barn. The barn was a bit bigger, and in it Tante kept a donkey for riding, and a cow and a goat for milk and cheese. She had a noisy rooster as well to crow her out of bed each morning,   and a speckled hen to lay an egg for her breakfast. With so many animals about, the tiny cottage wasn't tidy,   but Tante didn't fuss over a few feathers, a little fur, or a spiderweb or two.

Except once a year, when the days got short and the nights grew long the old woman would nod her head and say, "Time to clean for Christmas."

Then she'd shake the quilt and wash the window and scour the soot from the kettle. She'd scrub the floor on her hands and knees and stand tiptoe on her step stool to sweep the cobwebs from the ceiling.

This Christmas was just as always.

"Wake up!" said Tante, snapping her fingers. The dog stopped dreaming and dashed off to dig for bones beneath the bushes.

"Scat!" cried Tante, flapping her apron. The cat hid

under the bedclothes and the canary flew to the chimney top.

"Shoo!" scolded Tante, swishing her broom. All the spiders and each little wisp of web went flying out the door as well.

When she'd washed and wiped every crack and corner of the cottage, the old woman nodded her head and said, "Time to fetch Christmas."

Then Tante took the axe from its peg in the barn and hung the harness with bells upon the donkey. She scrambled onto the donkey's back, nimble as a mouse, and the two jogged and jingled into the fir forest. They circled all around, looking for a tree to fit Tante's liking.

"Too big!" said she of some, and "Crooked as a pretzel!" of others.

At last she spied a fir that grew straight, but not tall, bushy, but not wide. When the wind blew, the tree bent and bobbed a curtsey to the little old woman.

"It wants to come for Christmas," Tante told the donkey, "and so it shall."

She chopped down the tree with her axe, taking care to leave a bough or two so it might grow again. And they went home, only now the donkey trotted with the tree upon his back and the old lady skipped along beside.

The tree fit the cottage as snugly as if it had sprouted there. The top touched the rafters, and the tips of the branches brushed the window on one side and the doorframe on the other. The old woman nodded her head and said, "Time to make Christmas."

Then Tante made cookies. She made gingerbread boys and girls. She baked almond cookies, cut into crescents like new moons, and cinnamon cookies, shaped like stars. When she'd sprinkled them with sugar and hung them on the tree, they looked as if they'd fallen straight from the frosty sky. Next she rubbed apples until they gleamed like glass and hung these up, too. Tante put a red ribbon on a bone for the dog and tied up a sprig of catnip for the cat. She stuck bites of cheese into pinecones for the mice and bundled bits of oats to tuck among the branches for the donkey and the cow and the goat. She strung nuts for the squirrels, wove garlands of seeds for the birds, and cracked corn into a basket for the chickens. There was something for everyone on Tante's tree, except, of course, for the spiders, for they'd been brushed away.

When she was done, the old woman nodded her head and said, "Time to share Christmas."

Tante invited all the children in the village to come and see the tree, as she did every year.

"Tante!" the children cried, "that's the most wonderful tree in the world!"

When the children had nibbled the apples and sampled the cookies, they went home to their beds to wait for Christkindel. Christkindel was the spirit who went from house to house on Christmas Eve and slipped presents into the toes of their shoes.

Then the old woman invited the animals to come and share Christmas.

The dog and the cat and the canary and the chickens and some small shy wild creatures crowded into the cottage. The donkey and the cow and the goat peered in the window and steamed the pane with their warm breath. To each and every visitor, Tante gave a gift.

But no one could give Tante what she wanted. All of her life the little old woman had heard stories about marvellous happenings on Christmas Eve. Cocks would crow at midnight. Bees could hum a carol. Animals might speak aloud. More than anything else, Tante wanted some Christmas magic that was not of her own making. So the old woman sat down in her rocking chair and said, "Now it's time to wait for Christmas."

She nodded and nodded and nodded her head.

Tante was tired from the cleaning and the chopping and the cooking, and she fell fast asleep. If the rooster crowed when the clock struck twelve, Tante wasn't listening. She didn't hear if the donkey whispered in the cow's ear, or see if the dog danced jigs with the cat. The old woman snored in her chair, just as always.

She never heard the rusty, squeaky voices calling at her door, "Let us in!"

Someone else heard.

Christkindel was passing the cottage on his way to take the toys to the village children. He listened. He looked and saw hundreds of spiders sitting on Tante's doorstep.

"We've never had a Christmas," said the biggest spider. "We're always swept away. Please, Christkindel, may we peek at Tante's tree?"

So Christkindel opened the cottage door a crack, just wide enough to let a little starlight in. For what harm could come from looking?

And he let the spiders in as well.

Huge spiders, tiny spiders, smooth spiders, hairy spiders, spotted spiders, striped spiders, brown and black and yellow spiders, and the palest kind of see-through spiders came...

...creeping, crawling, sneaking softly...

...scurrying, hurrying, quickly, lightly...

...zigging, zagging, weaving, and wobbling into the old woman's cottage.

The curious spiders crept closer and closer to the tree. One, two, three skittered up the trunk. All the other spiders followed the leaders.

They ran from branch to branch, in and out, back and forth, up and down the tree. Wherever the spiders went, they left a trail behind. Threads looped from limb to limb, and webs were woven everywhere.

Now the spiders weren't curious any longer. They'd seen Christmas. They'd felt Christmas, every twig on the tree, so they scuttled away.

When Christkindel came back to latch the door he found Tante's tree tangled with sticky, stringy spiderwebs. He knew how hard the old woman had worked to clean her cottage. He understood how dismayed she'd be on Christmas morning. But he didn't blame the busy spiders. Instead he changed their cobwebs into a gift for Tante.

Christkindel touched the spokes of each web with his finger. The twisted strands turned shiny gold; the dangling threads sparkled like silver. Now the old woman's Christmas tree was truly the most wonderful in the world.

The rooster woke Tante in the morning.

"What's this?" cried Tante. She rubbed her eyes and blinked at the glittering tree. "Something marvellous has happened!"

Tante was puzzled, as well as pleased. So she climbed on her stool, the better to see how such magic was spun. At the tip top of the tree, one teeny, tiny spider, unnoticed

by Christkindel, was finishing its web.

"Now I know why this Christmas is not like any other," said Tante.

The little old woman knew, too, that such miracles come but once. So, each Christmastime thereafter, she did not clean so carefully, but left a few webs in the rafters, so that the spiders might share Christmas. And every year, after she'd hung the cookies and the apples and the garlands on her tree, the little old woman would nod her head and say, "Time for Christmas magic."

Then Tante would weave tinsel among the branches, until the tree sparkled with strings of gold and silver. Just as her tree did on the Cobweb Christmas.

Just as Christmas trees do today.

The Usborne Book of Christmas Stories